THE L▓▓ ▓▓▓▓ ▓▓ ▓▓▓▓ ▓▓▓ ▓▓▓▓RE

BY J.G. ECCARIUS

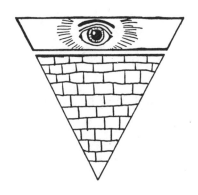

III Publishing
P.O. Box 170363
San Francisco, CA 94117-0363

1st Printing: December 1988
2nd Printing: January 1990
3rd Printing: May 1992

Cover Illustration by Chip Edwards
Cover Typography by Sammy Blue

ISBN 0-9622937-0-9

For God so loved the world, that he gave his only begotten son, that whosoever believeth in him should not perish, but have everlasting life.

— Holy Bible, John 14:16

I stand at the door and knock. If any man hears my voice, and opens the door, I will come in.

— Holy Bible, Revelation 3:20

And entering into the sepulchre, they saw a young man sitting on the right side, clothed in a long white garment; and they were affrighted.

And he saith unto them, Be not affrighted: Ye seek Jesus of Nazareth, which was crucified: he is risen; he is not here: behold the place where they laid him.

— Holy Bible, Mark 16:5,6

But a certain man named Ananias, with Sapphira his wife, sold a possession, and kept back part of the price, his wife also being privy to it, and brought a certain part, and laid it at the apostles' feet.

But Peter said, Ananias, why hath Satan filled thine heart to lie to the Holy Ghost, and keep back part of the price of the land?

Whiles it remained, was it not thine own? And after it was sold, was it not in thine own power? Why has thou conceived this thing in thine heart? Thou hast not lied unto men, but unto God.

And Ananias hearing these words fell down, and gave up the ghost: and great fear came on all them that heard these things.

And the young men arose, wound him up, and carried him out, and burried him.

And it was about the space of three hours after when his wife, not knowing what was done, came in.

. . .

Then she fell down straightway at his feet, and yielded up the ghost: and the young men came in, and found her dead, and carrying her forth, buried her by her husband.

And great fear came upon all the church, and upon as many as heard these things.

– Holy Bible, Acts of the Apostles 5:1-11

Chapter 1

THE BATTLE IS JOINED

Hobgoblins are the consistency of little minds.
- Professor Holbach

Providence is a quiet town. It has the aura of a grave-yard: life is a daylight interlude of sadness and calcula-tions of inheritance between nighttime orgies of witch-craft and tomb robbing. Official histories state that decay set in after World War II when competition from cheap foreign labor destroyed the costume jewelry industry, which itself depended on cheap Italian and Portuguese immigrant labor. But the truth is that when H. P. Lovecraft lived there in the 1920's the city was hardly more lively. More than one local sage has wondered if there might be some truth to Lovecraft's story of a Vampire entombed beneath the cellar of one of the pre-revolutionary houses along Benefit Street.

Professor Holbach liked Providence, which was quite unusual, since he was not a native. It was a comfortable place for him to live, with mild weather, affordable hous-ing, an Ivy League University, a few movie theaters, and a reasonable supply of lazy children from well-off families.

He was a tutor; Professor was only a nickname. His paying students were of two types: the rich, who could afford hand-holding the year round, and the middle class, who could afford only to cram for exams. He did not work at tutoring particularly hard; he worked only to maximize his free time and comfort. He did not make a great deal of money and needed to spend even less. He had no great ambition and was not particularly fond of adventure, having tried it and found it more annoying than exciting.

If he had known where accepting Cynthia Wass as a student were going to take him he would not have done it. He was compassionate, but he believed that trying to do too much good was prone to reversal. There was no warning. She appeared to be a nice, intelligent but unmotivated teenager good for fifteen dollars an hour in tutoring fees; that was all.

Cynthia had to cram year round in several subjects to have a fighting chance of advancing a grade level each year. Her parents wanted her to get a high school diploma before she was married off. Her father was from a twice-removed female off-branch of a wealthy Rhode Island family which had begun with piracy, advanced to the slave and rum trade, and then graduated to banking and manufacturing. He had not been overly well-endowed financially or mentally, but survived as a well paid, mediocre accountant in one of the firms that kept track of the family fortunes. Her mother focussed her intelligence on keeping her affairs from her husband's knowledge.

The Professor's sessions with Cynthia were not something to look forward to, but they helped pay the rent. If her parents had beaten her or psychologically or sexually abused her he might have taken a more professional interest; mainly hers was a case of dullness and lack of aspiration. For a while she had a crush on him and dressed up for the lessons, but that passed without incident. Then one rainy Providence afternoon she came in more attentive than usual.

"Do you believe in Jesus?" she said when she had the chance.

"Do you believe in Jesus?" he replied.

"Mary Avakian says she saw him. He talked to her. She says it's not like church. She says now she's happy."

The Professor twisted a strand of his beard with his fingers. "You never told me about Mary. Was she pretty unhappy before this happened?"

"Like most of us, only she . . . let a boy get her pregnant. Then her parents took her car and allowance away. So she started drinking and her grades went down and her parents got really mad at her and they were fighting all the time. But now she's stopped drinking and says she loves her parents."

"And Jesus just came to her all by himself? No one was trying to convert her?"

Cynthia's face turned inward for a moment before she answered. "This guy Paul. She met him by the Wall. There's some kind of church down in Fox Point, but she only went there once. Her parents won't let her go. Paul says she should obey them."

"Well. Whether you should obey your parents or anyone else depends on what they tell you to do."

"She saw Jesus. He talked to her."

"Have you ever had a hallucination?"

"No."

"It's pretty much like a dream, only it happens when you are awake or maybe only half asleep. You see or hear something that is not there. It starts happening regularly, psychiatrists call it schizophrenia and you end up in a nuthouse. There are a lot of causes, but in your friend's case it was from stress and depression. The dream or imagination circuits in the brain get shorted into the waking perception circuits. The reason she saw Jesus and not Mother Mary, the devil or her dead grandmother is because she was talking to this guy Paul. If she was talking to a Satanist she probably would have seen Lucifer."

"I guess. I never liked church except to see my friends. But I'm a Christian. I mean, everyone is a Christian. I mean, there really was a Jesus and all."

"Sure." Finding himself tempted to become vicious, he paused and entered a reassuring voice. "And there was a Mohammed and a Buddha. But that is no excuse for Christianity. Christians are always killing non-Christians and other Christians in the name of Christ. It's a sick religion. Be nice to Mary and I'm sure she'll get better of her own accord."

"Do you believe in God?"

"There isn't a God. This is a real world with real people and real problems. When someone gets killed they really die, they don't go to heaven, and when someone suffers they are really suffering, they aren't building up brownie points to please Jesus Christ. And, by the by, you really have a test on Friday and praying to Jesus is not going to get you a good grade. So let's hit the books."

On Friday Cynthia got a B- on her test with very little help from Jesus. She decided to humor Mary by going with her to the church. Mary's behavior had been so ideal that her parents had given her permission to see a movie that night. Jesus was more important to her.

Cynthia held Mary's hand tightly; she was as scared as Mary was excited. She had not been in Fox Point before. To her parents and friends it was a slum filled with thieves and rapists. In reality it was home to working Italians, Portuguese, blacks, and students, and had a very low crime rate.

Appropriately the church was located off Redemption Street. Mary led Cynthia down an alley between two old wooden houses towards a bare light bulb outside an unmarked door. The door was unlocked. Standing inside the Church of the Living Christ, they could see rows of folding chairs facing a pulpit. Three of the four people already in the church were black. Mary hugged each of them in turn, which Cynthia found rather unchurchlike. She was relieved that she only had to shake hands. They sat while more people drifted in announced by blasts of cold air. To Cynthia they seemed mostly old, but few were over thirty years old.

She did not notice the organ until it began to play. At that point there was no way to miss it. Attached to the front and rising above it, a glowing red neon sign said "Jesus" in foot high letters. Everyone was singing. Cynthia would have been terrified if Mary had not taken her hand again.

Three rollicking gospel songs later Paul, a tall, thin white man in his twenty-fifth year stepped up for a few Hallelujahs and Amens and to introduce the Reverend Bob. He was a barrel chested black man with a creased but unwrinkled face, a crew cut, and a short mustache. His voice was deep and solemn.

"Welcome to the Church of the Living Christ. We are gathered here for Love, not the love of mortals that waxes hot one day and wanes cold the next, not the love of the animal half of ourselves, but the eternal love of the Living Christ.

"There are people who will tell you all sorts of lies about Jesus Christ. They will tell you you must suffer. Have you not suffered enough? There is no suffering for the Living Christ. You won't find this living Christ in books, you won't find him in the churches of the rich or of the pious hypocrites. But if you open up your heart to Him He will come to you. Eternal love, eternal life! Many here can testify to this glorious truth . . ."

The rest of the preaching was punctuated by Amens and Hallelujahs from the congregation. The closest Cynthia had ever come to being in such a tide of emotion had been at school pep rallies.

She resisted, she was frightened, she thought them crazy, but the red neon JESUS pounded on her soul.

After an interlude of singing they all started shouting "Testify! Testify!"

A tall light skinned woman with red hair went to the front. "I was a prostitute," she said as if she were shouting Hallelujah.

"Tell it sister!" yelled a black woman sitting beside Cynthia.

"I was the lowest sort of prostitute. I was despised, I was desperate, there was no act I would not perform for money or drugs. My parents had beat me and my customers beat me and my pimp beat me. I tried to drown my sorrows in alcohol and drugs. Only they were drowning me."

"Then I met Reverend Bob, and he told me it did not have to be that way. He showed me the way to the Living Christ. He did not berate me or tell me to give up drugs or prostitution. I left those things behind after Christ saved my soul. Now I have eternal life and Christ as my guide. Now I don't need drugs and I have an honest job to earn a living. Sisters, I am saved."

The organ struck up "Spirit in the Sky." Cynthia was thinking how she was not happy, even though no one beat her and she kind of liked drinking and marijuana.

Almost everyone in the church testified, including Mary Avakian. Cynthia half expected to fall down on the floor and see Jesus as the chorus reached its climax. But it was over. She was introduced to Reverend Bob and then left with Mary.

A few days later the Professor should have known something was wrong when Cynthia did not try to evade her algebra lesson. Instead he attributed her increased concentration to the benevolent influence of his teaching methods.

After the lesson she looked straight into his eyes.

"He came to me," she said.

I don't need this, he thought.

"Jesus," he said.

"He's eternal life. I'll live in him forever now."

"What did he look like?" The Professor asked confidently.

"He was surrounded by light. He had very kind eyes and a beard and long hair. He said to lie down and keep calm, then he kissed me and I was filled with light. I was! And all the pain and sadness was gone. I'm free."

"Congratulations. I'm just curious. Do you remember what color his eyes were?"

"They were blue."

"And he had white skin?"

"Yes."

"I'm sure what happened to you was very important, but if you had been taken in by nuns you probably would have seen Mother Mary, and if it had been Hare Krishnas you would have been saved by Krishna. We know the historic Jesus was a Jew, and at that time Jews had not interbred with Europeans, so they had dark brown skin and eyes. Your mind manufactured its own salvation, and you won't really be free until you understand that."

"I love you Professor. Christ loves you. You'll see."

Seeing that she was temporarily beyond the reach of reason he gathered up his things. "Like the Pope loved the Albigensians. You aren't the first to try to convert me, so don't be disappointed if it does not work. I'll see you on Tuesday."

The Professor was only briefly disturbed by Cynthia's conversion. He had been brought up Lutheran, and having rejected that he considered himself immune to the more virulent forms of religious dementia.

He had met born-again Christians often enough, and once even spent a day at a Unification Church camp in California in order to see a cult from the inside. He had concluded that some of the sects were therapeutic. They took in social disasters created by sick parents and saved them, if not from hell, from drugs, brutality, and loneliness.

On his way home he walked along a street that ran through Brown University, which is to say over an ancient Native American burial site. He had two courses and two incompletes to go before getting his bachelor's degree in Sociology. He had not even attempted to take a course in three years. The thought that he could go back at any time, get his degree, and go on to become a professor, lawyer, doctor, or businessman reassured him that he had chosen the correct course in life.

"CIA out of Brown" was spray-painted on a wall, reminding him of the early seventies, when he had entered as a freshman and received A's in upper level courses. The rich could not even keep their own kids in line back then. But usually the bulk of students were conservative. Brown had educated Rhode Island's gentry for generations before football was introduced and Ivy League became a designation. With time it had become more of a national institution; in the 1950's it supplied the government with most of its CIA agents. One eccentric the Professor knew claimed the CIA's secret leaders met in the vast tunnel system that lay beneath the university.

He did not consider giving Cynthia up as a student. He tutored her four hours a week, sometimes more before exams. That alone paid the rent. Mainly he taught her what she could have learned in class despite the incompetence of some of her teachers. The advantage of tutoring for her was mainly that she could not sit daydreaming of flirtations and improbable romances in foreign lands. Also she could not pretend to be stupid; the Professor knew better. She had no problems with English, though she did not excel in it. Her mother, however, had indicated to her repeatedly that math, accounting, and her father were bores and a waste of time. Her resistance to math and science was quite high.

The Professor was seldom willing to believe that the slowness of some of his students was genetic. That was against his world view. He was willing to admit that if a fetus were exposed to alcohol or cyanide the organic brain damage would seriously impair mental function later in life, and rare genetic defects might have the same result. But, From his experience and reading, he thought most retardation was social in nature. Parents and teachers were infants' gods: a phrase from their lips could strike like a bolt of lightning, leaving a mortal permanently disinterested in (or afraid of) math, talking, genitals or life.

He did not feel social that evening. He ate at home, talked to his girlfriend on the phone, and refused an invitation to play cards. He watched some basketball on TV, listened to the Talking Heads album he had received for his birthday, and read several chapters of a book on Native American mythology.

When he went to bed he fell asleep easily. He liked to be conscious of his dreams and was a student of the writings of Freud and Jung. He regularly dreamed of his childhood or of such archetypal figures as the Old Man, the Charcoaler, and the Shrink. That night his dreams started in the house where he had spent his childhood.

Eventually he was walking up a spiral staircase in an old castle. He was going to get ice cream out of the refrigerator for his father. He found the refrigerator: it was tall, white and wide. He was not sure how to open it.

He remembered he had not said his prayers and knelt down. He made the sign of the cross and the door began to glow. Then its front dissolved into a pulsing red gate inscribed with the words "HUTE DIE WELT, HORT-LAK KANLI." A figure appeared behind the gate, dark skinned and brown eyed. It extended its hand. "Come with me," it said. "I am the Living Christ. Rest your head on my breast and join me in eternal incorruptible light."

There was something sinister about the apparition. "Mama, Daddy!" the Professor screamed, waking himself up. It was dark and the sheets were drenched in sweat. For once the heat in the apartment was more than adequate.

Clearly, he reasoned, it was an anxiety dream from his abandoning his parents' religion, and it had been triggered by his dealings with Cynthia. Still, he had seldom had such a vivid dream. He thought that it might have been interesting to go through the gate given that Christ was an illusion. On the other hand people went mad and became Jesus freaks somehow. The light of reason was counterweighted by the darkness of centuries past.

Providence is both sleepy and informal. People are apt to drop by for a visit unannounced; there is no need to buy an answering machine and set up appointments with friends two weeks in advance, as in New York City. The Professor wanted to get some outside perspectives on what had happened, and it was easy to arrange to have a few friends over the next evening.

Sophia was a girlfriend, a Greek American who had come from New York City to teach at a junior high school. Libby was a black leftist who worked at a shelter for battered women; she was his only close friend who had grown up in Providence. Jack had gone to Brown with the Professor, lived in Providence off and on, read a great deal, and dabbled in smuggling and muckraking.

After a suitable period of time catching up on minor gossip the Professor related his experience with Cynthia and the dream.

"It's pretty creepy, if you ask me," said Libby. "A lot of the women who come into the shelter are Christians, and it sure doesn't keep their husbands from beating them. It's just one more form of slavery. Pretty soon you won't be able to have an abortion. The Nazis didn't allow abortions, you know."

"Sure you've got your Falwells out there, but this particular incident hardly seems like a Republican plot," said Sophia. "Christianity has been on the wane since the French Revolution, but it's like drugs: it appears to offer something for nothing. But this born again Christian stuff seems on a different level, like hypnotism or some form of hysteria."

"My problem in understanding this," said the Professor, "is that Christ appears to be a sort of archetype. If I am right then it could appear with another name but the same effect. Everyone has seen pictures of Abraham Lincoln, but he doesn't appear to people and tell them what to do. Maybe Christ is part of the collective unconscious."

"Maybe in some sense Christ is alive," ventured Jack. "Christ is a pattern, maybe even a conscious pattern, that uses human brains as a host."

"A parasite," added Sophia.

"Don't you think you're getting a bit mystical?" said Libby. "And isn't that the problem in the first place, superstition and mysticism? I don't think that Jesus would still be causing trouble today if religion didn't serve the real material interests of the rich. Taxes, tithes and profits, sometimes I think we'll never get them off our backs."

"I don't disagree with you, Libby," said Jack, "but there is something more going on with this born again stuff. Maybe it is just an induced psychosis, maybe American bankers want psychotic Christians for workers. Maybe we should check out this church they're going to."

"No thanks," said Libby and the Professor simultaneously.

The Professor continued. "It's hardly the plague, and probably Cynthia will recover. Most important, I saw Christ in a dream and I'm still sane, so it isn't like a vampire is stalking people."

The discussion eventually shifted to other matters. The Professor was cheered because discussing the topic in a rational manner soothed his fear that his unconscious might be getting out of control. Just in case he slept with Sophia that night.

In his dreams he was back in his parents' house, sneaking downstairs to get ice cream. His father heard him and asked why he was up. He said to go to the bathroom, but instead he went to Cynthia's house.

"You don't believe in him," she said.

"He isn't real," he said.

"You don't have to believe in him. He is real."

"You don't need him to be happy." He noticed she was wearing green eyeshadow and heavy black eyeliner.

"But you do need love. Do you get enough love, Professor?" She came over to him, gazing seductively into his eyes. She sat down on his lap and kissed him. He pulled off her shirt and felt her sucking into his neck. He pushed her away, afraid they would be discovered, but she just said "You can have me, Christ is eternal life, everything is permitted."

He ran for the staircase but it was the stone spiral and he knew he did not want to go to the top. "I'm dreaming" he said, but he touched the walls and they were solid. He ran down the stairs and started to relax, for they were the stairs of his happy childhood dreams leading to a pleasant meadow.

He could see the gate to the meadow but there was a white freezer along the wall and he remembered the ice cream. He lifted the door. Inside, a bearded man in a gray three-piece suit beckoned him into his office.

"Yes, you can go far with us, Professor. You've had your problems in the past, but we would like your unique talents here. We are a rapidly growing concern. You can have money, power, women, complete research facilities and freedom to publish, whatever you want. And best of all, eternal life. Just a kiss on the cheek and you're in."

I've seen this before, something is wrong, thought the Professor. I don't want this job.

But he was mesmerized, unable to move. As the man was about to kiss him the Professor saw fangs behind the parted lips.

The Professor screamed, struggled, and awoke in Sophia's arms.

The next day he was walking on College Avenue and noticed that Paul was there, preaching to a small group of people. Most were cynical Brown students amused at his rantings.

"... is not the answer, money is not the answer, drugs are not the answer. None of these can give you eternal life. Jesus is the Answer."

"Excuse me, sir," said the Professor.

"Yes?" responded Paul.

"Are you talking about Christ the Vampire?" said the Professor.

"What?"

"Christ the Vampire. He was a magician in ancient Palestine. The Romans tried to kill him." The Professor noted the confused horror in Paul's face and the amusement and disgust of different onlookers. "Only they didn't know to drive a stake through his heart. So he has lived ever since, appearing to people who are weak. Whoever accepts his kiss gets sucked into the whole trip and becomes a mindless zombie wandering around trying to suck in the living by saying things like 'Jesus is the answer.'"

"Lucifer, this man is possessed by the devil," screamed Paul, pointing his finger at the Professor.

The onlookers were exiting quickly. The Professor had not anticipated the violence of Paul's reaction. He said very calmly "You'll get better if you stay away from the other zombies."

He walked away, purposefully casual but very aware in case Paul should attempt a physical attack. He was able to contain his laughter only for the distance of half the block. But as Jack had said, "If you could kill that vampire with laughter alone Voltaire or Twain would have done him in."

Chapter 2

33 A.D.

Holding a Central Committee meeting is always dangerous. Our movement, at this stage, would certainly be destroyed if the Italians captured its leaders. It would be more dangerous to not hold a meeting: at critical times like this the only way to forge the necessary unity is through face to face discussion. It's like walking down the street: the people following you and the people headed towards you could be assassins, but most likely they are out shopping.

There could be a police agent on the Committee, but if you kicked out everyone you ever suspected there would not be a Central Committee. Today if you had to guess it would certainly be Peter, but more likely the pressure has just gotten to him and he is scared. Everyone always suspects Thomas because he argues so much. His anarchist tendencies are a real problem, but that hardly makes him a police agent. The funniest thing is that he suspects Judas, the only person beyond suspicion. He can be trusted with anything.

"What's on the agenda?" said Philip, always impatient to start.

John started the reports. We had still had no success influencing the Palestinian Liberation Army's military and political strategy. However, our work with them was influencing their troops; several have deserted them and joined us.

"Unfortunately," said John, "we suspect some of them of supporting international revolution because it means they don't have to fight in the meantime. We have to be careful or we may be accused of being counterrevolutionary by the PLA."

Aside from the usual problems, there was one that was major, if anticipated. Some informants, servants to the Roman imperialists, reported increasing concern about the miracles and the size of the crowds we are attracting now.

As planned, Mark introduced the critical item. "As you know we are having great difficulty getting organized outside of Judea. You also know the importance of the cultural front given the strength of the Romans. Right now Jesus is the only person who can perform miracles, and we know how difficult it is to train a magician who is politically reliable. Even if all Judea rose up against Rome they would crush us. They've already proven that. We have to get beyond nationalism, we have to have an international revolt. The only way that is going to happen is if we send Jesus to organize and teach outside Palestine."

The moment he was finished half a dozen voices tried to speak in opposition. Naturally Thomas ended up speaking first. "This goes against our principles. Yes, Rome can only be defeated by the peasants and slaves of the producing nations. Yes, we must change the very souls of men if we are to set up a Godly, communal society. Yes, Jesus is our founder, leader, most skilled orator and magician. Others will oppose this plan because it seems to put him in even greater danger. That is not my point; weakness puts us all in danger. The point is that this plan goes against the very nature of what we are trying to do. Can we defeat Rome with magic? They have magicians as good as Jesus. Can Jesus make legions disappear?"

"We will defeat Rome the only way it can be defeated: with arms. To do that we must first defeat them with understanding, with class consciousness among the peasants and workers. Miracles gain their attention, they do not increase their understanding. That is gained through experience, argument, and study. We need to recruit fighters, and to recruit them we need orators and teachers. We cannot free God's children, we can only teach them to free themselves. We must be prepared to carry on even if Jesus is killed tomorrow. We are not much better off if he performs miracles in Athens. It makes the people look to Jesus for salvation instead of to themselves. That is enough of a problem here."

While a majority of the committee agreed with our position in advance, that is no guarantee that the argument won't go against us. In such a matter unity is crucial. We win largely by persuading Thomas's faction that we agree with him, but that I am capable of getting things going outside Judea without resorting too much to magic shows.

On most important questions one side consists of the brothers who are oriented to politics and the other side is more oriented to culture or religion. It is usually easy to get the decision I want, but it is harder to get the needed understanding.

So I will leave for Alexandria soon enough. An equally critical matter takes place at dinner when no one is expecting it. The wine is mildly drugged to help open their minds. It is time to try my new invention, the slogan. It is like a political prayer or mantra. Anyone can say it or yell it; you don't have to be a skilled orator.

I have only to wait for the general conversation to work up to a proper pitch of anger and energy.

"A toast for the people," I say.

I focus my mind. We are together.

"Bread and wine for the people!" say the disciples, echoing my words.

"Blood and death for the Romans!" For this they are even more enthusiastic.

When I am alone with Judas, John and David the inner nature of the slogan can be revealed. "The body can live for a much longer time than most people think, but a long time is not forever. A soul, however, can spread itself out among several bodies, thus remaining alive even if a particular body dies. But each body has an effect on such a soul. To remain ourselves we must inhabit bodies that think proper thoughts and take proper actions. Then we can influence such bodies.

Bread and wine are necessary for life: one is the body and the other the spirit. We must battle the evil ones of Rome. Among them the Illuminati also know these things. We will win because they cultivate a refined few and we will refine a cultivated many. Someday humans will have one soul, and this will correspond to a society that has no oppression or exploitation. Then we will all be ready for union with God."

A little understanding, but not too much. Most people, though, you could tell everything, they are so stupid.

The Prime Illuminatus was submerged in a marble bath. Only her face and nipples broke the steaming water's surface. Some said she had not aged in two hundred years. Others said she was a spirit and her body an illusion. Some even claimed she transferred herself from one young body to the next.

When she spoke to the Agent her voice echoed in his skull as if it were a half dozen voices in close harmony.

They were in Rome deep beneath the Coliseum. The Agent was intensely aware that he was beneath an altar of human sacrifice and that the reward for good work was balanced by the fate of those who failed.

"This Jesus," the Prime said. "I thought he gave up illuminism and religion for politics. Now you interrupt my meditations to say he is a threat to the Empire. Organizations like the PLA are troublesome, but hardly worth my attention. Any Senator is more dangerous than the PLA. And if Jesus really is a threat why not just kill him?"

"It is a very complex problem or we would not bother you with it," said the Agent. "He is in religion and politics, he hates Rome and Illuminism, which is not too unusual in the provinces. The PLA is a danger to stability in Palestine, but hardly looks beyond it. Jesus was with a splinter group called the Zealots, the ones who carry out all those assassinations, stabbing Romans in the back in the streets.

"But he is more than just a fanatical Jew. He formed his organization. It is referred to as the Brotherhood. It is supposed to be a religion centered around him being the son of the Jewish God. They call him the Messiah. There are always half a dozen would be Messiahs running around Judea. The dangerous twist is that he claims to be the god of everyone, not just the Jews. According to our informer he wants to unite all the peasants and slaves of the Empire in a revolt; the religion is largely a cover. He's a rather competent magician, of course."

The Prime interrupted her. "Do you really think he practices magic just to destroy Rome? Do you think someone with such powers cares about slaves?"

"Perhaps not," said the Agent. "But they have set up cells now in a dozen or so cities. They are not a danger yet, we could arrest them all tomorrow, but you can see that a revolt of all the provinces would be much more difficult to deal with than any one revolt at a time. The religion is just a front for anti- Roman politics."

The Prime considered that Jesus's aim was just the opposite: politics was a vehicle to allow him to put himself in place of the Illuminati. In that case he might be somewhat difficult to kill.

"So where did this Jesus get his training? Has he been in any of our schools?"

"We believe he has travelled and studied extensively. He spent three years with the Essenes, a year in Athens, two years here with Christos, and then he disappeared for five years. Some of his ideas could have come from the Buddhists and Magi, but he is secretive even with Judas, our informant, so we don't know if he actually travelled to study with masters or if he learned them second hand."

"How close is Judas to him?" said the Prime.

"One of the closest, considered totally trustworthy."

"And what does he think Jesus is capable of doing?"

"Judas says Jesus claims true enlightenment can only be achieved by all of mankind at once, and that requires social equality and universal education."

"That is a quaint combination of Judaism and Buddhism. Nevertheless, this Jesus could be even more dangerous than you think. Arrange to have him killed, and if at all possible by the Jews, not by the Romans. But do it quickly."

"Yes, my Prime."

"Just as important, Jesus may know the Secret of Life. However he is killed his heart must be destroyed."

"And the others?"

"Don't kill them, at least not yet. We may be able to make use of them. Count Piso has an idea for dealing with the Jewish problem."

"It will be done."

When Jesus was arrested it was no surprise except for the timing. They would have been wise to wait until he was some place where his abduction would have escaped public notice.

The show trial was a surprise; not that the comprador bourgeoisie, the Pharisees and Sadducees, had ever been anything but enemies, but that they would publicly condemn him for Rome.

Of course he could have escaped, he was one of the world's best hypnotists, but that did not suit his purposes. It was time to defy death, not by dancing around it, as many of the old ones had, but by absorbing its power into himself.

Everything seemed to be going fine during the crucifixion. He withdrew into his inner regions, slowing his metabolism and readying for death, knowing his disciples would pull him down and minister to his sleep. But he sensed, just before he fell into the void, a danger. It was a Roman soldier, a private, and he was hefting his lance. It was easy to read his mind: he was going to aim for the heart.

The Master called out to the soldier, but was without his normal powers. The soldier felt a cold fear, but he was already thrusting the lance forward. It struck below the Master's right breast, smashing a rib and puncturing a lung.

The disciples had not expected this. Three of them, James, Carl and Joseph, had been given careful instructions, including to expect him to rise out of death. They had even been warned that it was possible he would not live, and how to carry on in that event. Now they stood looking at the Master, filled with sadness and anger, cursing Rome and its posterity for eternity. All they could do was wait until the Jerusalem police let them take the body. The squad of Roman soldiers withdrew almost immediately, certain that Jesus the Pretender to the Throne of David was dead and would soon be forgotten.

Carl now directed the removal of the body. They carried the Master six kilometers to the place that had been prepared. On the way nothing distinguished him from a dead man; his heart could not be heard to beat, and he did not breath. The only thing unusual was that his body was very cold, colder than a corpse would have been. But that was no sign of life.

In the cave dwelling carved into the cliff of Sarah's Hill an argument immediately ensued between Carl, James, Joseph, and Thad the Egyptian. James and Joseph did not want to touch the wound, because that was not in Jesus's detailed instructions. But Thad and Carl argued that Jesus must not have foreseen the attack with the lance, and that perhaps their enemies knew the Master was not to die. Therefore they too had to compensate. Finally Carl started washing the wound with boiled herbal water, settling the debate with action. Meanwhile the lamb's vein was readied and the boy Isaac was brought in. As soon as he had finished with the wound Thad inserted the vein with a silver needle into

Isaac's "third" artery. The other end held a gold needle that was inserted into the vein in Jesus's neck.

The warm blood only made the body colder. Thad knew this was a good sign; Jesus's metabolism was using its energy to repair the damage and to summons the Powers of Death. When the boy fainted Thad disconnected the vein. The boy was Jesus's son by Mary; only Thad knew that Mary was Jesus's sister.

Only now did they anoint the body and wrap it in cloth. In the burial chamber the disciples prayed in total darkness. They ended with the ritual of the communion of minds, and those that were adept could feel the now passive mind of the Master. So he lived. His body was placed in a special box made with three layers of wood and metal. Four men sat watch in the pitch blackness after the others left.

Each hoped the Master would sleep past the end of the watch. They knew the legend. When the Master arose, he would be thirsty.

Chapter 3

THE CONVOLUTION OF JOHNNY TYPIC

When she woke up in the morning her first thought was generally, "I can't believe it." Everything had to be done, nothing was what she wanted to do. She had to get dressed, had to eat breakfast, had to walk to the bus stop, had to talk to her friends, had to go to her first class.

At the age of sixteen Johnny Typic's most characteristic emotion was hatred. Like many teenagers she was smart but green: she knew about the world only from her own environment and a selection of books, magazines and television shows. She projected her feeling of powerlessness and oppression into everything. There was little she could do about it except to hate what appeared to be the world's sources of evil.

She did not realize that she had no right to feel slighted by the wheel of fate. She lived in a house that was luxurious by world standards and about average even for United States citizens. She had to share a room with her sister that might have housed a family of six anywhere else in the world. She was well fed by any standard of history or geography. Her parents had never beat her or sexually molested her. She had a stereo and looked forward to driving a car. She was even attending a private, Catholic school though her parents could not really afford it.

Despite this she hated. She hated her mother most of all. Mother was the most powerful figure in her world. At the same time mother was powerless, a housewife whose sole purpose in life, as far as Johnny could tell, was to make her miserable and force her to become like the sick people who populated the world. Mother was Catholic and was sure Johnny was Catholic too. Johnny was an atheist, but never said so. She was not absolutely sure that there was no Creator, but she was sure that

Catholicism was out of touch with reality. She believed in sex, birth control, Darwin, and the equality of women. She listened to punk music when her mother was not home. She would have rather committed suicide than become a housewife or a Catholic.

She hated her schoolteachers less than she hated her mother only because each one individually had less power over her. She especially hated the nuns, who she referred to as ducks, for dried up cunts. She hated social studies class most of all, and was suspected of heresy by the nun she hated the most, even though that sister believed that women should be allowed to be priests, and was known to have signed a petition to review the Church's dogma on birth control. Johnny figured that one thing dangerous about the Church was that it had no scruples. She had read up on its history in the public library: she knew about the Crusades and the Inquisition. The Church still used its power in a country like Italy where they were in the majority, but were smart enough to act moderate when they were in the minority or were losing some of the flock.

She hated Ronald Reagan because he was the master of the art of being mean while acting nice. She really hated America but was not really able to say it even to her self. She felt herself an expert at recognizing hypocrisy. She knew that South Africa was not a democracy and Nicaragua was, more or less, and knew any nation that really cared about democracy would be giving money and arms to the black South Africans, not the Contras. She knew Reagan hated women because he was against abortions. The sight of him on TV infuriated her.

Her father was lower down her hate list only because he was not around very much. He was in a position to seem more reasonable than her mother; he was not responsible for disciplining her. She did not realize that her mother was the way she was partly because that was the way Father wanted Mother to be.

If Johnny was not reasonable at least she balanced her hatred with a bit of compassion. When her teachers picked on some student Johnny sympathized with the suffering soul. The further away from her in time and space people were the better she was able to sympathize with them. Partly this was because they were poorer and more miserable; partly because the arts of literature and journalism picked out the nobler or at least more intense and universal aspects of people's lives.

In short, Johnny was a typical American teenager. Her parents were typical American parents: they had only a faint idea of what was going on in her head.

On April 29 something strange happened. When she stepped of the bus there was a crowd of students centered around some people she could not see who were yelling. Then she remembered seeing the leaflet, something about World War III, with the date April 29 on it. A man was screaming about induction and war in Europe and patriotic duty. Sister Mary Jesus Joseph was threatening to suspend anyone who did not go into the school immediately. Johnny's friend Rose said the men were Vietnam Vets Against the War and were pretending it was the Day Before or something. A punk in a mohawk handed them leaflets.

"Let's go with them," said Mark, a reputed heretic.

"Father Imbroglio endorsed it," said someone, which made it less attractive in Johnny's eyes.

About twenty students and punks were leaving with the men dressed in combat fatigues and gas masks. Most of the others were headed towards the school building, but over a dozen milled around harassed by the Sister, in a state of indecision.

"We'll get in trouble," said Rose.

"I think we already are," said Johnny, for Sister was heading towards them like the centurion ready to spear Christ. They fled towards the school.

As soon as she could she went to the girl's room and read the flier the punker had handed her. It had a picture of sheep marching up to and forming a mush-room cloud. Words and phrases like "Riots not jobs," "Be all you can be, sign up now for world war III," "debts," "crisis," "Trident," and "nuclear winter" were scattered in different typefaces over the page. At the bottom it said "They won't listen to reason, Stop the governments from launching World War III, No matter what it takes!" There was also an A with a circle around it; she had seen it before but did not know what it meant.

She had thought plenty about nuclear war, how stupid it was, how it fit the world she lived in perfectly. Society was mad and obviously someone would push the button someday and it would be all over. The idea of world war was strange, out of history books, masses of psychotic men killing each other with rifles and tanks. It was something spread over time, years, but nuclear war would be over in minutes or at most days. And how could anyone prevent an unreasonable government from launching World War III? No Business As Usual, the flier said.

During the day people talked about the incident, a little about the vets and nuclear war, but mostly about how much trouble the people who left would be in. Piecing together the gossip of the day Johnny got a strange picture: several people who went had already been in trouble for anything from punk hair to cutting classes, but a couple were nobodies and two brains went, Kelly and Gordon. If the brains had not left the others might have been expelled, but Johnny figured they could not be expelled so everyone would just get demerits, which meant almost nothing. The parents would be called and some of the students would be grounded for a while.

"Which is democracy in America," explained a woman from Brown University at a meeting a few days later. They were in a Burger King not to far from the high school. "You have formal freedom of speech, they can allow that somewhat because the information you receive is so controlled most people never think to say anything that is dangerous to the system. Look at the daily papers and news shows here, they did not mention No Business as Usual Day except for a tiny paragraph buried in the Journal that called it an anti-nuke protest, did not mention World War III, and did not even use the phrase No Business As Usual."

There were four adults at the meeting: the Brown student, a man who identified himself as a Vietnam vet, a woman wearing black like a punk but maybe thirty years old who identified herself as an anarchist, and a black woman who was clearly the heavy and invariably used words like "proletariat" or "revolution" when she talked. Everyone else was a teenager, some were punk and some were straight and most were women. Johnny only recognized one person from her school, Kelly, who was a star student and reputed good Catholic.

"I think we should talk about doing a No Business As Usual Day again soon," said a boy who looked younger than Johnny and had black hair rising straight up from his skull to a height of about an inch. "Most people didn't really know about it until after it happened. A lot of kids at school were talking about war the next day and we all think it looks bad. If it takes resistance to stop them from launching war we had better keep doing this. I'll bet two dozen people from my school would come next time. We could do it once a month and really disrupt things in this town. If you just did it once people would think it's just a weird form of an ordinary demonstration and then wouldn't take it seriously."

A number of other teenagers affirmed the sentiment, then the Brown student spoke. "I think we should definitely make people more aware of the danger of World War III and plan some future actions. The best way to do this, however, is to talk about the world situation and get some consensus on how dangerous the situation is. Then we should talk about what different kinds of people are thinking, and how to get them thinking about stopping the government from launching World War III. Once we have some unity about what's going on and where we are at we should have no difficulty deciding whether the next step is handing out pamphlets, having a fundraiser, blockading the streets again, or all three."

The meeting went as Blade planned. In the end it was decided that three people would write a flier saying what happened on NBAU day and why it was urgent that a resistance movement be formed. Two people would look for a place to show a movie for a fundraiser and everyone would help distribute the leaflets when they were printed. There would be an action, a march or something, as soon as possible, and interested people would meet to plan it the following Wednesday.

Johnny wanted to talk to Kelly after the meeting but instead was waylaid by a totally punked out woman calling herself Cinder.

"I didn't see you on NBAU day," said Cinder.

"I didn't know about it until I saw the Vets in our school yard, and then I almost went. I wish I had."

"We're going to go have some fun, me and Joey and probably some friends. You should come. We have a can of spray paint. Lets split before the RCP lays into us." They were already out the door.

"The RCP?" inquired Johnny.

"That paper, the 'Revolutionary Worker,' the Vet sold you is their paper, the Revolutionary Communist Party. They are OK, I like Blade and all, but I'm not a communist. I don't want anyone telling me what to do. I'm an Anarchist. Hey Joey this is Johnny. She's coming with us."

The knowledge that she was walking with Anarchists and had just been in a meeting with Communists put her in a mild state of shock. Johnny didn't say anything again or listen closely to her new friends until she found herself in an apartment somewhere in Smith Hill.

Throbbing hardcore rock music of uneven tempo decorated a room painted shock pink and counter-pointed with assorted mostly black objects: a lamp, table, mattress, panther skin, and art on butcher paper that frequently spilled over onto the walls. One of the paintings looked vaguely like Jesus Christ except it had vampire like fangs instead of a smile. Joey noticed her staring at it.

"That's Christ the Vampire," he said. "Cinder painted it. There is this guy Jack who told us about it. Christ is really a vampire, that's why Christians act so stupid and cold. They're his victims, like zombies."

"Christ the Vampire," said Johnny. "And the Holy Inquisition. There should be a band."

"It's true," interjected Cinder. "He really is a vampire. That's how he rose from the dead. That's why Falwell and Reagan jerk around like puppets on a string: they really are. Tonight is the night of the living dead and it's been going on for twenty centuries. Watch out honey, Christ the Vampire wants You."

Cinder was so serious Johnny was scared. Fortunately a yet unintroduced male sank his teeth, gently, into Cinder's neck, causing her to scream and the room to burst into laughter. In the course of a cursing the would be vampire turned out to be called Louis.

"That's why I like the Bolsheviks. They wiped out Christianity virtually overnight," said Joey.

"Yeah, and sex and anarchists," said Cinder.

"You don't know what you're talking about" said Joey. "The Bolsheviks were accused of being anarchists by the Marxists in Germany because Lenin was against bureaucracies, and also they were for sexual freedom. You have to distinguish between Bolsheviks and Stalin."

Louis, not wanting to go though another anarchism versus communism argument, intervened. "Christ the Vampire is going to do us all in. Christians have infiltrated the armed forces of the US and SU and England and France and are taking over the nukes because Christ is telling them they can go directly to heaven when the Apocalypse starts. My brother told me, he runs a computer at an ICBM base in South Dakota. He got drunk one night when he was home on leave and spilled out."

"Your brother is a Christian?"

"Everyone in my family is a Christian, only the others are just your usual brainwashes. Christ doesn't have to fuck with them personally, they're just going through the motions. My brother though, he's in personal contact, personal control, the Vampire has him good. He has to control all the people who are needed to launch the nukes."

"That's not how it works" said ever serious Joey. "Capitalism needs Christianity. It's part of the system to keep people lobotomized. There's a contradiction because Capitalism also needs Science; when Christianity gets out of hand it can slow up technology and production. Right now they're revving up Falwell and the anti-abortionists and women-on-their-back-ists because that's what they need to prepare people for World War III."

"World War III, World War III, I'm tired of World War III," complained Marion whitefaced and blackhaired. She bounced up and down to the Crucifucks' mad music and then leaped backward onto the bed with her arms and legs akimbo.

"I think I had better go home. My parents are going to kill me." That Johnny was under her parents control irritated her but was a convenient excuse to not deal with the weirdness.

"World War III staring you in the face and your parents are going to kill you if you don't sleep peacefully."

"Sleep peacefully, sleep peacefully, sleep peacefully," shrieked Marion from the bed.

"Is she on drugs?" asked Johnny quietly.

"Drugs are for amateurs," quipped Joey.

"The world is insane. We are totally in touch with reality," said Louis.

"Let's get out of here," said Marion. "Spray paint will save the world." She seized a can and held it up with the tips of ten fingers as if to show the gods.

Outside they debated the merits of various slogans and walls. For the most part safety, the likelihood of not getting caught, stood in contradiction to effectiveness, the number of people a slogan would reach. This debate was also over Johnny's head, for the motley crew seemed to know the merits of each location. Would someone remove the paint and how quickly, were there likely to be people around at this time of night, were there good escape routes if the police saw them? She did not dare announce that she hoped they would go to her neighborhood; she felt it was too late to walk alone.

Johnny's thoughts of getting home led directly to the idea of having to explain this to her parents. This caused her to envision shouting and restrictions, to wonder what it would be like to say what she had really done and what she really thought. They did not even know she did not believe in God; how would they react to her being a communist or anarchist?

When Johnny came out of her reverie Marion was spraying a circled A in red on a mail box. "It's supposed to be black," she said to Johnny as they walked away "but Joey got the paint and he always gets red."

They came to a Catholic Church, Saint Stephen's, and Louis demanded that they stop. The others spread along the block, ready to alert Louis. In less than a minute "Christ the Vampire wants You" was spread across the stoney face of the church. Johnny fled with the others down the street. They did not stop until they were blocks away.

"That's great," said Louis. "Those stones are porous as hell and they can't just paint over them. They might be able to solvent blast it off, but that will take days."

"World War III, we're on the fucking edge and you're worried about the frigin Christians," complained Joey.

"O.K. 'Civil War, not World War,' is next" said Cinder.

But on the stone wall along Chalkstone Boulevard Joey wrote "World Revolution, Not World War." Everyone was getting irritated and paranoid because he took a long time to write in big letters.

"Look guys, I have to get home. Can we walk to my house?" asked Johnny.

They really did not want to be walking around too much with the Providence police out looking for vandals. Cinder and Louis offered to walk to Johnny's home; the others headed back to the apartment.

Johnny's mother was sleeping on the sofa and did not wake up when Johnny came in. "Where've you been?" said her sister when she came into the bedroom.

"Just talking to the people at that meeting."

"Mom's pissed. She's gonna kill you."

"I'm already dead. What more can they do? Fuck them."

"You shouldn't talk like that."

"Don't be stupid. Go to sleep."

Johnny was still awake when her sister's breathing had turned regular and shallow. She would not have to deal much with her mother in the morning, there was not enough time before school. Her mother would tell her she could not go out, maybe for a week or two. She would get a lecture. Maybe the virginity lecture. She mocked her mother in her thoughts, whining "Your virginity is the most precious thing you can give a man when you get married."

Her usual fury at Mother's stupidity was compounded by the idea of nuclear war. "The most precious thing you can give nuclear war is your virginity." She imagined Providence as vapor. She remembered her school teachers saying that the reason there had not been a real war since World War II was that both sides would be destroyed by the nukes. She thought about wild west duels, both men knowing they might die, and shooting it out anyway. She thought about Nicaragua and Afghanistan. She thought about her parents who had voted for Reagan and thought the faster the US built nukes the more assured the peace. She considered everything she could think of and could only conclude that insane people run the world and there was no way to rule out nuclear war. She wanted to ask the No Business as Usual people why they were so sure the war would start soon.

Having exhausted one subject she briefly thought of her new friends. They were weird, but she liked them and wished she could run away and live with them. She wondered about Christ the Vampire. It was a funny idea, but it went against her rational inclinations. People were Catholics because they were taught by Catholic parents not to think, to have faith instead. If Christ were a vampire then Hindu parents would have Christian children; the parents would not be able to teach their children to think like Hindus. Unless it was like the vampire movies and the vampires were limited. Living death: that certainly described her parents.

She found herself walking along a street and looking at a wall that said "Keine Weltkrieg" and suddenly there was a blinding light and she turned around to see a mushroom cloud ascending to the heavens, glowing churning with blackness. She was thinking in German, trying to picture some escape route, but there was none. She was going to die, perhaps was already dying, but was not dead. Johnny returned to wakefulness, startled by the reality of the dream. Had she been a German woman dreaming, or had the war started in Germany, or had her mind made it up? She got up and looked out the window, but it was a normal, quiet Providence night.

Laying down again she worried about people who see Christ. Were they just hallucinating? Having a waking dream? Once one of her friends took LSD and told her about the bizarre hallucinations she had. How could she know what was hallucination and what was real? What if she took LSD and saw Christ the Vampire? What if she went crazy and became like her mother?

She began to wonder how her mind worked. They had studied the brain in biology, but that was not very helpful. Cortex, neocortex, hypothalamus, dendrites, synapses. The information came in through the eyes, ears, nose, ran along nerve cords, and somehow was dumped into her consciousness. What she really sees and hears is electrical sparks, nerves firing, adrenaline, so they must be a pattern reflecting chairs and tables and faces. Only what sees that, more nerves? Where does it end? She imagined looking down at the earth, and looking into her brain forming an image of the earth, and then she was rushing back from the earth, seeing the sun and other planets but all the while looking into a tunnel looking into her brain, rushing back and seeing more suns come into focus, jumping back from the brain and seeing an infinity of brains peering at everything imaginable, turned inside out as the galaxy crystallized for a moment and rushed away to be joined by others, meshing into cell-like membranes around empty space, infinities of awareness opening into infinities of awareness, zooming and opening into nothing, infinite in infinite directions.

Chapter 4

THE POPE

He did not realize the true importance of his mission until he learned that the Pope would see him immediately after lunch. It was common knowledge in the Roman Catholic Church that the Pope talked to God during lunch. There was no doubt that they would be talking about the Christ the Vampire problem, which he referred to in his mind as "the sacrilege."

Bishop Jello was quite disturbed that the contagion had broken out in the Diocese of Rhode Island. He had felt sure he was due to be promoted to Cardinal; now such promotion would be contingent on his success is solving the problem.

Decades of abstinence from exercise and women combined with the necessities of running the Church in the most Catholic state in the nation had pinched the Bishop's face inward near its center and bloated it outward around its periphery. His eyes appeared beady because of the mass of flesh around them and his mouth, whether frowning, smiling, or, more likely, hanging in idiotic passivity, conveyed a self-satisfied hypocrisy.

It was no coincidence that the Pope and Reagan had both been wounded by assassins and survived in an almost miraculous fashion, but Bishop Jello was not thinking of this. He wanted to put the situation in the best light, and yet cover his ass, in case the problem proved beyond his abilities to solve. As his steps drew him closer to the sitting room he began to wonder how the Polish Pope would see him.

The Pope was dressed in a mass of starched white cloth drapings, a altar boy's wetdream. Without makeup on his face he looked two decades older than his television image. Yet he looked kind. Grandfatherly. Bishop Jello was taken in only for a moment: his mind snapped back to its normal devious piousness as he mumbled the usual greetings in Latin and settled into a chair that left his eyes a good foot and a half closer to sea level than the pontiff's. He had no choice but to look up at the wilting kindness of god's sales manager on earth.

"Well?" said the Pope.

"Well?" echoed the translator.

Actually, the translator upset Bishop Jello more than anything else. He stood a few feet from the Pope in a confluence of shadows, black flesh wrapped in black robes and nothing but a black shadow discernible inside his hood.

"We have a problem," ventured Bishop Jello.

"Yes, I have read reports, but I would like to hear it in your own words," said the Pope and Translator.

"Apparently there is a plot in Providence to teach everyone that Christ is a vampire. Of course that is totally, not only profane but beyond reason. Apparently the center of this plot is one Professor Holbach, who is not a professor at all, merely a tutor. In any case punks, punk rockers have been painting such messages on the walls and talking to and corrupting schoolchildren. Apparently they are also involved with communists and anarchists. It is weakening the faith."

"And so what measures have you taken?" said the Pope.

"The police have arrested some of the people in question, and they have received brief terms in prison. We have gotten the community on notice so that the slogans are taken down as quickly as they go up. But the real problem is that some of the children are having bad dreams. We are giving them counseling, but I fear a wave of hysteria. It could hurt the image of the Church if the newspeople took it up."

"Do you believe in Vampires, Bishop Jello?"

"No, I do not."

"Do the faithful in your diocese?"

"Many people have fears even when they consciously reject such an idea."

"Do you think that Jesus Christ our God is in any way like a vampire? Would the people think that?"

"Only in that he lives forever."

"But to live in Christ forever is to be in heaven, is it not?"

"Certainly."

"There have always been people who question the faith, and there always will be. Think of it as a test."

"There is one other thing," mentioned Bishop Jello.

"Yes?"

"In America there are many Protestant sects that believe in a personal appearance of Jesus to someone, they call this born again Christianity. These attacks seem to be aimed at them as well, and may have been precipitated by such an incident."

"Very good. This is what comes of protestantism. You must not directly attack our fellow Christians, but it would certainly be good to argue that Catholic priests are specially ordained to intercede with Christ."

"Yes, your Excellency."

"Cardinal Vlad will want to talk to you about certain practical matters concerning this. I can see you are a man of great faith, and will serve the Church well. Use your own judgement, but keep us informed. The Devil works in strange ways; we cannot rule out yet that this is such a case."

Bishop Jello was determined not to let the Pope's easy manner and flattery bring his guard down. He had not heard of Cardinal Vlad, and he did not like talk about the Devil. Otherwise he felt the interview went well. The Church had weathered worse attacks over the centuries; and he felt the truth was on his side, for a change.

It turned out he would not be able to see Cardinal Vlad until the next day. The young priest who served as his translator and guide offered to take him to tour the city of Rome, but the bishop preferred to retire to his quarters. It troubled him that his guide could not only not tell him about the Cardinal, but believed he must have gotten the name wrong, having never heard of such a man. Worse, at dinner his enquiries about the Cardinal were met with stoney silence.

He had a copy of Newspeak magazine in his room and forced himself to read it. He did not generally keep up on the news; he was agitated, and not accustomed to finding tranquillity in the Bible. When he had finished reading it was still too early to sleep. He turned on a radio and listened to classical music. It was only then that he took note of his surroundings. The walls and floor were made of a white stone that was not marble, but the ceiling had been plastered over. Three paintings hung on walls: one of the Virgin Mary, one of Jesus, and one of a man who had doubtless been a Pope. It occurred to Bishop Jello that each painting was centuries old and might be worth tens of thousands of dollars or more.

To his delight he at last began to feel sleepy. He turned out the electric light and turned the radio to a low volume. He waxed angry for a moment at the people who had mocked his faith and imagined various forms of dealing with them, including ones he had heard of the Mafia using. He grinned thinking how easy it would be to persuade the Don to defend the Faith. Then he had the comforting thought that Cardinal Vlad was with the Inquisition and usually worked outside of Rome. That would explain why Bishop Jello's guide did not know of him, but that the older functionaries at the dinner table were afraid of him. A man to be careful with, but doubtless he would know how to deal with the vampire people.

The music was still playing when he was half-awakened by the opening of the door. He could not open his eyes, but there was light in what had been a pitch black room. A faint rustling approached his bed; he clutched his sheet in fear.

"There is nothing to be afraid of, Peter." This in a low voice smooth and rough as well aged whiskey.

He opened his eyes, but at first could see only a bright flickering light.

"I hope you don't mind being awakened, but I did not realize you would begin your sleep so early."

In the bishop's consciousness the light resolved into a candle. Behind it was a black figure, a man in a black robe. The bishop raised up his head, but could not see a face inside the black hood of the robe.

"I am Cardinal Vlad."

"Pleased to meet you." The bishop sat up in his bed. Now he could see a aged white hand holding the candle and traces of a face inside the hood.

"We must have our talk. Please put on your vestments and come with me."

"Certainly, Cardinal."

The Bishop was scared but still half asleep. He felt as if he had been thrust back into the Middle Ages. It was the robe: it was a monk's garment, not that of a Cardinal.

"This problem, you see, is an old one. You must not make light of it, but do not underestimate our power to deal with it, either. That is fine. Just your shoes now, we must take a walk."

They went abreast out into the hall. At the end of the hall was a staircase which they descended. The Bishop felt as if he were sinking. He tried to think of something to say to break the ice, but could not.

At the bottom of the staircase a hall led in one direction towards the Pope's quarters and in the other towards the Curiate. Instead of going either way the Cardinal opened a large wooden door inlaid with bronze. They descended another stairway.

Now the Bishop realized that the Cardinal was still carrying the candle. It was in a rectangular lamp of glass and metal. There was no other light in the staircase, but every second turn on the way down there were halls that were lit.

At last they came to the bottom of the stair. Here the hall was not lit. The stone was rough rather than finished. The air was damp and had a fungal smell. The Bishop was afraid, but trailed along after Cardinal Vlad.

"Where are we going?" he asked after they had walked far enough to tire him.

"We are going to a special Mass to pray for the quick resolution of this plague. It is to take place in the Lateran Cathedral. We are going there through an ancient underground passage in order to avoid detection. Right now we are still beneath the Vatican City."

The Bishop tried to get a glimpse of the Cardinal's face as they walked, but the hood covered it so that only looking at him head on would have worked. He did not see how a mass would help, but at least it was a familiar idea and helped to relieve his anxiety.

"It was such a surprise to have such a thing happen in my Diocese. My flock is very faithful, especially for Americans."

"The faithful must be tested, Peter."

The Bishop reflected that he might have become almost anything if his name had not been Peter. But being named after the first Pope had given him confidence that he could serve God. From altar boy to the priesthood, that childish bit of confidence had helped him through the doubts and trials of his career.

A sound brought him out of his reverie. Alerted, he focused on it. It was not there. Then he heard it again: it was a groan. Fear returned to him. He could see no change in the Cardinal, just a steady walk. The Bishop heard more groans. As they walked the groaning merged with a high pitched wailing.

Were they torturing people, thought the Bishop in a panic. Was he being taken to be tortured? Surely the Church no longer did that. The silent faces of dinner loomed before his imagination. Vlad the Inquirer, he thought.

They came to a cross tunnel and turned right, leaving the sounds of misery behind. Perhaps, thought the Bishop, he had imagined it, or it had been the sounds of the streets above muffled through the ground.

Suddenly the walls receded. The candlelight formed a circle on the ground, but otherwise the darkness surrounded them. The Cardinal walked calmly forward. Now instead of inspiring fear the black robed figure was the Bishop's only hope.

The sound of running water came from in front of them. The Bishop became calm enough to try to estimate the size of the cavern they were in; he thought they must have walked fifty yards already.

"Be careful here," said the Cardinal.

Suddenly the sound of rushing water was beneath them and the circle of light upon the floor had narrowed to a couple of feet across. The bishop halted; he had almost stepped over the edge. The cardinal went ahead.

"Wait!" cried the Bishop.

The Cardinal turned, but was only a shadow in the darkness. "Have you no Faith?" he said. Then he turned around and walked on.

The Bishop did not mind not having faith so much as he minded being left alone in the dark. He walked quickly to catch up. He realized he had lost face with the Cardinal. He thought cynically that it would have been easier to have Faith if he knew the passage as well as the Cardinal.

The bridge over deadly waters was just behind them when the Cardinal sank out of sight. Edging forward the Bishop could see that there was another descending stairway, with a flicker of candlelight quickly fading. For the first time in thirty years he said a heartfelt prayer to Jesus asking for deliverance.

Finally catching up to the Cardinal and the light he found himself confronted with hideous corpses, mere skeletons with leathery flesh hanging on them, eyes pits of black above silenced screaming mouths. The Bishop sank to his knees and hence into darkness.

He was disturbed by demons swimming up from his inner mind — thousands of boys and girls terrified of their sexual organs, old ladies frozen in hysterical robotic patterns of hypocrisy, longings for the flesh interwoven with hatred of the flesh, classes of dying minds chanting "Yes Sister Mary Joseph," donations made to appease businessmen's consciousnesses, investments in slum housing and corporations grinding millions of human souls into profit, coldness staring into coldness — his consciousness came crawling back to the candlelight seeping through his eyelids. He did not want to open them. Even if all he would see were the cloaked face of the Cardinal and the lifeless remains that hundreds of thousands of tourists saw each year while touring the catacombs.

The sudden weight of a rat running over his belly brought him to life.

He let out a piggish squeak and moments later was hugging the Cardinal's skirt. "Must we go this way?" he pleaded. "Is it much further?"

"Bureaucrats," said the Cardinal in disgust. "We cannot expect saints, but surely we could find men with more faith to govern the Church."

"It's the darkness, Cardinal. I'm not used to walking in such darkness."

"Perhaps you cannot handle this. It would be very bad for the Church if this evil spread. Perhaps we should send a special envoy to eradicate this cancer."

"It's a question of how you want it handled," said the Bishop. "If the ringleaders were silenced then the rest would quiet down."

"And how do you propose to silence them?"

"They could be run out of town, or warned, or killed. I think warning would be best. A good beating might convince them that there game is not worth playing."

"Do you think people possessed by the devil will stop their evil doings just because of a beating?"

"I doubt they are possessed by the devil. We are watching them. They do not appear to be satanists. They think it is just a prank."

"Then where did this idea that Christ is a Vampire come from?"

"I see. You think they are inspired by the devil, perhaps without knowing it."

"And the others," said the Cardinal, "why do they believe it and spread it? The very children in your own Catholic schools."

"I think children have a streak of perversity. There are always some that challenge the authority of the Church."

The Bishop began worrying again when the Cardinal did not respond. Had he said the wrong thing? He had not had time to think; he had been honest. Should he have attributed the whole thing to the devil? Would he be relieved of the bishopric, or watched over by some inquisitor? He was lucky, he thought, to have avoided a heart attack or falling off the bridge.

In this moment of deep doubt and self criticism he did not realize he was following the Cardinal up another flight of stone steps. Only the quickening of his heartbeat, his labored breathing, and tiring calves pulled him back to his immediate surroundings. His eyes had finally adjusted to the darkness; he could see around himself very well. Now there were just stones and more stones, halls and more halls, steps and more steps, pain and more pain. Once in a while he would stop to try to catch his breath, only to panic as the Cardinal receded from sight.

Bright lights shone from above. The Bishop expected to emerge into the familiar Cathedral, but instead found himself in a room about the size of a small parish hall. It was illuminated with about a dozen candles. At first all he could make out were six dark robed figures in addition to the Cardinal and a large, unornamented altar.

As his eyes became accustomed to the light he noted too that the priests or monks were humming. He could not identify the music; it did not sound medieval or modern. But more disconcerting than its odd harmonies was the room itself. It had no entries save the one he had come up through. The walls, floor, and ceiling were solid marble.

The altar was made of the same stone. It was unadorned, but a chalice sat on it and a cross hung on the wall behind it. The cadence of the humming quickened and the Cardinal began to recite the Mass in Latin. The Bishop could not listen; it hurt too much to kneel on the stone floor.

He could not see the faces of the humming monks. They did not respond as the congregation should to the mass; instead they continued humming. The Bishop realized he should be answering the Cardinal's prayers, but felt funny about breaking the spell the monks were weaving through acoustic space. He expected the Cardinal would be staring at him in reprehension, but could not see his eyes in the dark shadow of the hood.

He figured the Cardinal and Monks must be from a special order, perhaps one created by the Inquisition. They knelt in two rows of three, facing each other, just in front of the altar. At an appropriate point the Bishop stood so as to relieve his knees, but this made him aware that the ceiling was only a few inches higher than his head.

No longer concentrating on his knees, the Bishop started paying close attention to the Cardinal. The sounds weaved into the humming and into the Bishop's mind, suspending him and making his body fade away to abstraction. The words were clear:

"This is my body, take it and eat!"

Bishop Jello followed the Host upward over the Cardinal's head. Now for the first time candlelight penetrated the hood and reflected back into the Bishop's eyes from the Cardinal's face. From his stance ten feet away the Bishop could see only blackness where there should have been eyes and only skin where flesh should have covered bone.

He was as paralyzed as a bullfrog caught with a flashlight and about to be speared. Even as the Host was lowered back to the altar his mind went to war, the greater part denying what he had seen and the rest unable to forget. The words of the mass continued and in his hypnotized state the Bishop thought they came directly into his mind rather that from the impossible lips of the Cardinal. Each seemed filled with meaning, with the implication of the whole weight of Catholic dogma, of heaven, and of hell.

Without thinking, unable to enunciate internally, the Bishop anticipated the coming Communion. Surely he would die before the Host could reach his mouth. Surely God could not have ordained such things to come to past? He felt as if he were watching a movie, half asleep, with the music and words coming in through earphones, filling him with childish terror.

The acolytes began moving for the first time since the Mass began. Three went behind the altar and three before it. The Cardinal's voice carried an edge of excitement.

The black robed monks were pushing on the top of the altar. What had seemed a solid stone now obviously had a heavy slab top, a quarter of a meter thick, which slid slowly to the Bishop's right. It moved steadily until it was almost halfway off the altar.

"Do this in memory of me!" ejaculated the Cardinal.

The Bishop felt pulled towards the altar. He stepped forward without appreciating it; it seemed as if his camera eyes simply zoomed into the interior of the altar. The monks had reached inside and were turning over what at first the Bishop thought was a fleshy, waterlogged corpse. Turned on its back it appeared to be a mature manlike thing with long hair and a face so overwhelmed by fat as to obscure its features.

One of the monks carefully poured the dark, thick contents of the Chalice into the mouth of the creature. The Bishop could see that the monk, like the Cardinal, had no eyes, and perhaps no brain behind the eye sockets. This no longer seemed strange to him; he was tranquil as the monks hummed their deathless fugue.

They waited patently as subtle signs of life began to appear on the face. The music grew more intense and the eyes opened, first a slit, and then, slowly, to fullness. The grey eyes were unfocussed at first but then looked around and found the Bishop's face.

"Who is this man," he whispered in Latin.

"May I present Bishop Jello of Providence," said the Cardinal. "We have a serious problem in Providence."

"Yes, I know," said the creature.

"I thought it would be easier to handle the problem if he became one of us."

"Yes, he must become one of us. Look into my eyes, my Bishop, for you are about to see in a new way."

The Bishop looked straight into its eyes and the room faded away, but the music played through his mind and the void was filled with the Cardinal's words echoing Latin, Greek, English, and Aramaic: "This is Christ, Eternal Life, The Holy Spirit, Forever and Ever, Till the End of Time."

Waking he did not want to open his eyes. The meaning of the previous night was clear. He did not want to see the altar, to know what lay inside it. Then he noticed that he was laying on something soft, not stone, and that he did not feel like what he thought the monks must feel. Cautiously he opened his eyes and saw the cheery surroundings of his bedroom. Cautiously he lifted his head; he felt fine. He went to the mirror and saw his familiar eyes shining back at him rather than two lifeless pits.

After a few moments of happiness he was beset by confusion and anxiety. Even if he had not become a vampire there was no facing the horror of the memories.

He could not go on; he must run away and hide somewhere far from Cardinal Vlad. But he did not know how to earn a living, and he had no money of his own. He decided he would leave immediately for Providence, gather what church funds he could, and fly to somewhere pleasant and Protestant. Australia might not be bad.

There was a knocking on the door and his guide entered the room. "Good, I see you are up already," the guide said. "I trust you got a good night's sleep. Breakfast has been prepared and Cardinal Vlad will see you. My friend Felix says the Cardinal is a very kind man and you are quite fortunate to be able to see him. If you are ready, I will show you the way."

Bishop Jello felt sick and frightened but resigned himself to his fate. "Let's go," he said.

They walked to the refectory but entered a private room to the side. The guide left the Bishop there with a small table set with two chairs and covered with fruits, cheeses, breads, and pastries. Though he was hungry he had no desire to eat. He did note that the sun was coming through a window in the wall. He did not believe the Cardinal would actual come into the room. Rather, there was an inner door, and he expected to be summoned through it.

The door started to swing open and the Bishop froze. A cardinal entered the room, smiling. He was a medium built man, and despite his age showed none of the flabbiness common to celibates. His eyes were bright blue, his hair blond and grey.

"Good morning," he said. He had a French accent.

"Good morning," replied the Bishop.

"I'm Cardinal Vlad," said the Cardinal, and extended his hand.

Such was his confusion that the Bishop shook the Cardinal's hand rather than kissing it. The Cardinal overlooked the mistake.

"I understand you have problems in your Diocese. The school children in particular are being infected by some sort of hysteria about our Lord Jesus Christ being a Vampire."

"Yes, your excellency, and it has gotten progressively worse. It began with a young joker, an atheist and cynic, who began telling the punk rockers that Christ is a Vampire. The Punks started telling the other kids this and even spraying "Christ the Vampire" on walls. More and more children are having bad dreams about Christ being a vampire."

The Cardinal managed to smile and look serious at the same time. "Yes, that is a serious problem, and it must be confronted. It is not surprising that the children would get hysterical and start having dreams. The Faith is not what it used to be, especially not in the United States. When the priests and even Bishops, and you know who I mean, doubt the authority of the Pope, how can we expect the Children to not become confused? Every day they are exposed to people who believe in Abortion, who support atheists and communists, who talk about Democracy as if it were possible to vote on the Word of God. Tell me, do many of your priests tolerate abortion and birth control in their congregations?"

"Most will not admit it, but even if they preach against these things it is hard to police the flocks. Only a few in my diocese will publicly say Catholic women should use birth control, but many are silent on the issue."

"And what about Nicaragua? Do many support the Sandinista government?"

"Quite a few, but not as bad as in, say, Boston. Many more are neutral, saying Christians must be for peace."

"You must clean up your Diocese. If the priests do not accept and promote the Church's position they must be relieved from public duty. We must end this confusion in the Shepherds, and that will end the confusion of the sheep. We must reinforce the position of the Church and the Authority of the Pope. Then the confusion of the flock will fade. You understand the Church's position on Nicaragua?"

"It would be good if you would clarify it for me."

"We support the Contras. The Sandinistas are atheists and are giving the peasants and workers material goods in order to insure that they go to hell in the afterlife. Many priests are supporting the Sandinistas because the poor are better off materially and they cannot see the danger to their souls.

"Officially we are for peace, to be arranged by power sharing between the Contras and the Sandinistas. In reality we desire to restore a capitalist, pro-American government. We have no love of America, but Capitalist atheists are happy to have the peasants be Catholics.

"When you return to America you should make the Church's position clear to the priesthood in your Diocese. With regard to the parishioners and public, we support the Contras, peace, and democracy against the totalitarian Sandinistas. Is that clear?"

"Yes."

"With regard to the Vampire hysteria, children who succumb to it must be isolated from the others until they recover. More time must be spent promoting an image of Christ that is loving, compassionate, and merciful. You say that there is a conspiracy to spread this. Do you know who the conspirators are?"

"Most of them. Certainly the important ones."

"They must be discouraged, if necessary silenced. Do you know how to do this?"

"The police would look the other way if we roughed some of them up. If it were necessary to do serious harm to them, there are people in the community with those skills."

"Don't go to the Mafia. We don't want to owe them favors. Surely there are men in the Knights of Christianity United for the Faith who can be trusted."

"Yes, there are those who will help."

"One more thing. The United States and the Soviet Union are both planning to launch a world war sometime in the near future, according to our intelligence sources. We believe hundreds of millions, perhaps even billions of people will die. This will cause people to see the devil inspired nature of both Capitalism and Communism; it should be possible to unite the world in the True Faith after the war. You should quietly prepare your people to survive the war. If you need help Cardinal Zucconi can tell you what is necessary."

"Yes. We must protect our flock. But should we not warn people?"

"It would not avert the war, and it would put us at odds with the U.S. government, which is not in our interest at this point. I'm sure you will understand, upon reflection."

"Yes, you are right."

"You are not hungry?"

"I'll take a piece of fruit with me. I must get back to America."

"It is a pleasure meeting you. I am confident you can do what needs to be done."

The Bishop was relieved that his vivid experience had only been a dream. He had a moment of panic when the sun hurt his eyes as he walked to the limousine, but then recalled that he had been inside in dim light for over 24 hours.

Chapter 5

INTO THE NIGHT

The Professor did not think much of ambition, but he occasionally amused himself by thinking he was brilliant. Since he was only twenty-six years old he supposed he still had time to fathom some previously unfathomable aspect of reality, most likely in psychology or sociology. He mainly worked towards this by reading insightful books, which he would have done anyway, since it passed the time in a safe but stimulating fashion.

He did not believe his realization that Jesus Christ was the archetype for vampires was brilliant or even important. This was fortunate, as the idea of writing an essay to publish his ideas terrified him. At some date he might study vampire mythology, collecting in his mind signs that various writers had recognized the connection but were afraid to state it, but he could never write down his findings for the world. He wanted to be a Hegel or Jung, and failed to realize that even they started their work and gained their fame with lesser insights. But then, he was only amusing himself.

He was not particularly interested in the Christ the Vampire legend, and was somewhat embarrassed that Jack and the punk rockers had taken it up with a vengeance. Several times he had seen people trying to scrub the slogan "Christ the Vampire wants You" off of walls, and this made him chuckle. He knew, however, that certain interests would be pissed, and went out of his way to avoid the teenagers who somehow knew that he had invented the legend. He saw Jack about as frequently as ever, which was almost never.

When Jack showed up one Saturday morning he signalled that something was up by greeting the Professor by his first name, Richard. Despite this they talked briefly about each other's health and the weather as tea was prepared. When they sat down with steaming hot tea to drink the Professor was just finishing relating how he had suffered a minor injury playing basketball.

"Well," said Jack, "It could be worse. Two of my friends got beat up pretty badly last night."

The mere thought of pain disturbed the Professor. "How did that happen?" Part of him did not want to know, and another part of him was curious. He held the teacup to his lips in case the answer was unpleasant.

"It was Jaimie and Steve. They were out and decided to mark up a wall up near the hill. Some men jumped them, knocked them down, kicked them. Steve had a rib cracked and Jaimie lost some teeth."

"I guess people aren't too happy about spray paint."

"They didn't say 'That will teach you to spray paint on public property' as they left. They said 'Cut the vampire crap if you know what's good for you.'"

"What could you expect from Christians," said the Professor, pretending to dismiss it. He was both nauseous and very conscious: imagining being beaten, defenseless and at the same time recalling the terror and anxiety of childhood in which he was praised for being good (following orders) and punished for being bad (not following orders). All this had been rationalized by the sufferings of Christ on the Cross and the need to lessen them by his following orders. Speaking of love the adults had taught hate, speaking of justice they rationalized their own slavery. As a teenager he had delighted in a secret sort of rebellion, reading books his parents and teachers were too ignorant to know mocked their religion, God, and customs. He had wanted to commit sacrileges, to be excommunicated, to prove that hosts don't bleed when torn apart even in front of a congregation, to utterly embarrass his parents. But he had simply left home and let his wounds heal.

Jack realized that Richard had fallen into a reverie. He waited patiently, recalling the story that Socrates had once remained in such a reverie standing at a roadside for three days.

"I suppose you are going to tell me that they will try to get us next," said the Professor.

"It's a safe bet."

"It's not like I've been preaching from street corners. They probably don't even know I exist. And I'm willing to bet you can take care of yourself. After all, they are only human."

"Pardon me, Professor, but you do live a rather secluded life. We are talking about major interests here, and not just the church. These people ruin lives when petty loans aren't paid and put people in prison for stealing insignificant sums of money. They screw everyone and everyone hates them. The myth of Christ is incredibly valuable to them. It makes the society controllable. We might be puncturing that myth as it has never been punctured before. We don't believe in vampires or Christ, but people who believe in one tend to believe in the other. They can't risk letting this get out of hand, and it might if they don't take action."

"Why me? I just wanted to study. I just wanted to shut up a man who was preying on a child. I don't want to be involved."

"Have you seen your car today?"

The Professor answered by way of dashing to the window. From there he could see his 1966 Plymouth Valiant. It had not been stolen as he had feared. The windows had been smashed.

"I'll kill the motherfuckers," he said.

"That's the spirit, but realistically you are severely outnumbered. A more reasonable goal would be to get you out of the state alive. Preferably before nightfall."

"I can't just leave," the Professor whined. "I don't have the money, and all my stuff, my books, my records."

"It will do you good. Anyway, we don't have a choice, except maybe all hanging out together, and even then they would find a way to get us. Think of it as guerilla war. You won't read about it in the *New York Times*, but if we keep moving and spreading the vaccine around, if you will, it will get to the point where we don't count. It will be in the hands of the people, and there will be hotheads and egomaniacs willing to step forward and become targets for the powers that be. If we want to be forgotten we will be forgotten. But first we have to get out of here alive, and then we have to kick up some dust."

"I guess I should pack."

"Pack light. Some of our friends will be coming over later, so you should get a couple of them to go with you to your bank. Also call your parents and everyone respectable you know; the Christians are less likely to move if they think it will double back on them."

"How will they know?"

"If your phone isn't tapped someone is derelict in their duty. I have to go make a few arrangements. Some other people are leaving, and they are going to be gathering here. I'll tell you about the travel arrangements when I get back. How much money do you have?"

"Seven, eight hundred dollars."

"That will have to do."

The Professor watched Jack leave and immediately decided not to join Jack's cultural guerilla war. His first thought was to order new glass for his car, but he realized it would just get smashed again unless he left town. He had always claimed he wanted to travel. In actuality the idea of coping with a foreign culture frightened him. This he considered proof that he was not fit to help start a guerilla war. After all, they would be harassed wherever they went, and they would be outsiders.

Obviously he had to pack, but even that was problematic. He did not know where to go, or whether to go by car, plane or train. The prospect of landing in a city and immediately having to find work did not appeal to him. It takes time to build up a tutoring practice. He began thinking of people he might go and stay with, which triggered memories of past adventures.

The doorbell rang. The Professor immediately wished he had a gun, and, better still, some skill in using it. He considered not answering, then carefully looked out the window to see who was there. It seemed to be a young man; beyond that he could not tell. He decided to go down and talk to the man from behind the locked door.

It was a teenage boy, probably, with a mohawk combed down to either side so as to pass for normal, if one only glanced at it.

"Professor! It's me, Joey. Jack sent me over to help you out."

The Professor could not recall seeing the youth before, but decided it was safe to open the door.

"Hi. Look, Jack was wrong in presuming I would go with you. I have other plans. I'm sure you'll do fine without me."

"Uh, sure Professor, that's no problem. Do you mind if I wait for the others here? We were going to meet here, and most of the others don't have phones or are out getting ready."

"Alright, come on in, you shouldn't be hanging out in front of the house."

So they went up the stairs and the Professor retreated to his bedroom and closed the door.

This behavior did not do much to reinforce Joey's confidence. He was not convinced by Jack's arguments that the Christ the Vampire campaign was the only hope to prevent world war. If he had not just been purged from the Revolutionary Communist Youth Brigade, Providence Branch, for thinking for himself, he would not have considered it.

Joey had been warned by Jack to not expect too much from the Professor, but it still seemed like a bad start that the man who had initiated the Christ the Vampire story was not even going. Would the awakening of millions of Christians, particularly youth, create the cultural conditions for revolution in the U.S.A? It seemed more likely they would all be killed before they could even spread the myth.

If he had not been determined to leave Providence anyway, he probably would not have been there.

As Joey looked at the Professor's books and the Professor tried to decide where to flee to, Marion was walking the streets, in disguise, looking for Rapmaster Blue, who was now known mainly as just Rap. When she could not find him in the allotted time she went back to her home to pick up her bags and get over to the Professor's.

Rap was waiting outside her door, blaster blasting. "Hey Marion, Sheila told me you were looking for me, so I came by. Looking to book this super DJ for an extra fancy Party? I got the voice, I got the beat."

"Jack wants to know if you want to help give some Christians an ass kicking. Personally, I could live without your bull."

"I heard about Jaimie and Joey."

"It was Jaimie and Steve."

"That's too bad, if anyone deserved divine retribution it was Joey. Look, I'm with you, but I have better things to do than to rumble with the Knights of Christianity United for the Faith."

"That's not what we're going to do. We're going to split Providence and start telling people about Christ the Vampire. We're goin to travel. It will be super rad."

"That's capital corn, but not for me."

"Well, Jack wants to talk to you. He said you're attached to your records like . . . I forget. A drag queen to her jewels, or something."

"I got the hottest collection of riffs north of Harlem. I have oldies, goldies, blues and news. I will bid adieu to number 2, being the prisoner of gesture that I am. Where is the man?"

"Come on, he's at the diner. Let's hurry, we have to be out of here by nightfall."

Back at the Professor's the doorbell rang, rousing him momentarily from his stupor. Joey went down to let in Digger. Joey was polite, but he did not think highly of Digger. As usual Digger was in his colors: multi-colored tie dyed shirt, generic jeans patched in multiple hues, a black hat, assorted buttons, and the dead head skull button. Joey disliked Digger because he was resolutely non-political and pro-drugs.

Digger did not particularly like Joey either, but, as a semi-official representative of peace, love, and understanding, he did not allow himself to show it. "Hey Joey, I didn't expect to see you here, what's happening?"

"Getting ready to travel. What are you doing here."

"Came to see the Professor. Jack invited me. I'm going to lend my karma to eliminating vampires. You know the Professor?"

"Yeah," was all Joey could manage. He turned and started up the stairs. There was no way he was going to spend a portion of his life stuck in a van with Digger. In fact, he decided not to go.

At the top of the stairs he turned responsible. "Look, Digger, if you have any drugs on you don't bring them in. The police are probably itching for a chance to beat us up and arrest us in the process."

"Yeah, sure, cool, Jack told me. Pot and acid aren't addictive, I can fine without them."

They went in. "So where is the Professor?" asked Digger.

"Behind that door. He says he isn't going."

"Are you going?"

"Maybe. I figure I'll watch over the Professor till Jack gets here."

"I think I'll go in and say hello," said Digger.

"Suit yourself" said Joey.

The Professor was standing looking out a window, but turned as Digger came in.

"Hi Professor, what's happening?"

"Hi Digger. You caught me at a bad time."

"That's OK Professor, everyone has bad times. It will pass. It can't be that bad."

"You heard what happened to Jaimie and Steve?"

"A serious drag. I can't believe people are like that."

"Visit a war zone. Hell, take a look outside. They smashed up my car, and that is meant as a warning? And what did I do? I pointed out the obvious. Of course I didn't expect people to spray paint it all over Providence."

"Well," said Digger "liberation can be painful. But what are you going to do? You can't stay here."

"I guess," said the Professor "I'm going to go to the airport, fly to San Francisco, and hope my friend Melinda will let me stay until I can get back on my feet. Maybe someone can ship me my things. The rent is paid until the end of the month, plus I have a deposit down."

"That sounds great Professor. I'm going to San Francisco when this trip is over. It's still a real happening city. Give me Melinda's number and I'll look you up when I get there. Oh, wait, I have some friends there in case Melinda doesn't work out."

"Thanks Digger. Are you going on this trip with Jack and Joey?"

"Hell yes, it will be a blast. Of course I don't have to, I haven't had anything to do with this vampire stuff yet, but it will be good to travel."

"So it's just a free ride for you."

"No, look, I'm a Digger. You know about the Diggers?"

"Sure, I've heard of them, in England during Cromwell's time. They believed the land belonged to the laborers, right?"

"Right, but they also believed in Digging into things. Finding out. Curiosity. That is the essence of spirituality. So that is what this trip is. Christians are truly messed up mentally. Maybe we can find out why. We can change it."

"They've been around 2000 years. You aren't going to change them. By definition they are people who don't change. And you know Christ is a vampire only in the figurative sense."

"Sure, but when it gets dark you aren't going to be safe. So I'll put on some music and you call the airport to book that flight to San Francisco. O.K?"

Digger assessed Joey as he chose an album and set it to spinning.

"You're looking a bit glum for the vanguard of proletarian revolution. And I can't believe the party would let you go on this trip."

"I'm not in the RCYB anymore, and I'm not going on this trip."

"Who is going?"

"Jack, Cinder, Marion, Johnny, and maybe Rapmaster Blue and Libby. Why the hell are you going, anyway?"

"Because I'm a crazy."

"What do you mean?"

"Generally speaking, doing new things is dangerous. The first person to explore new territory is most likely the first to die. But if the human race did not constantly adapt to new situations it would be extinct. So society produces crazies, I don't know how. We do dangerous things that most people think are crazy. That's how society makes progress."

"Like the Long March."

"The what?"

"The Long March during the Chinese Revolution. If the Communists had not been crazy enough to do it, Chiang Kai-shek might still be ruling China."

"Sounds like a fine example to me. Look, since the Professor is leaving tonight we might as well pack up his food to take with us. Can you help?"

"Sure, that's fine."

While they packed Johnny considered how to escape from her room. Her parents had caught her packing, surmised what was happening, and physically confined her; she had a black eye to show for the struggle. She could have gone out the window, but they would have seen her just as if she had walked down the stairs. She could wait until they were asleep at night, but by then her friends would be gone. She could not even get to the phone.

She really wanted to go. Her parents had been even more down on her lately than was normal. She was being harassed at school, mainly by her teachers, but by some of the students, too. She was getting ready to run away from home anyway, either to Marion's or out of town, when she heard of the trip. She had asked Jack if she could go.

She considered setting off the smoke alarm, but could not see how that would get her by her father, unless she could go out the window while he was fooling with it. It was not likely to provide enough time.

Gazing out the window again across the gardens to the opposing set of row houses she wished she could fly. She was afraid to go out into the world by herself, but she knew she would rather die than stay at home. There had to be some way.

The way was up. She realized she would have to climb out the window and up onto the roof. Then she could cross to the next house, in fact to the end of the block, and let herself down. It was possible that one of the neighbors would see her and call her parents, but they might not, and all she needed was a few minutes head start.

She slung a bag of her most essential belongings over her shoulders and carefully let herself out the window, backwards. She could stand and put her hands over the edge of the roof, but did not think she had the strength to pull herself up. She went back inside.

She wanted to burn the place down.

Once it occurred to her it did not seem like such a bad idea. A bit drastic, to be sure, but something that her parents richly deserved.

She quietly opened her door. Judging from the sounds downstairs her father was watching TV and her mother was in the kitchen. She went into their bedroom and turned off its smoke alarm. Then she crumpled some notebook paper and stacked it in the corner where a wooden bureau met the wall. But then she could not bring herself to light it.

I'm too well trained, too fucking repressed to do it, she thought. Then she remembered how difficult it was to get a fire started in a fire place. It was not likely that the paper would cause the wood to catch. Which meant her father would be running down the block after her in a matter of seconds.

She went back to her room and got a candle. She set it in with the paper, knowing that it would melt and then create a fine blaze. She lit the paper and returned to her room.

It seemed like forever. Finally the fire alarm in the hall started beeping. She opened her door and stepped into the hall as her father ran up the stairs. For good effect she screamed as she looked at the fire in the bedroom. Her father rushed in, quickly retreated before the heat and smoke, and ushered them out of the house.

Neighbors gathered, some using garden hoses to wet down the outside and their own houses. Within minutes the fire engines began to arrive and Johnny simply walked away from the confusion.

Rapmaster Blue and Jack heard the fire engines in the distance as they dined at the Silvertop. Blue was important, though not indispensable, to Jack's plans. He was far more talented in communicating than the others in the group, and he was black, which meant he could more easily enter into certain communities and roles. Jack did not have a plan for recruiting Blue; he knew how difficult it would be to manipulate an honest man.

"Look," said Jack, "you know what the stakes are better than anyone. America's empire is falling apart and there aren't any signs that we are about to enter a period of peace and prosperity. You could be the bard of this era, but not in Providence."

"Into the Valley of Death rode the six hundred. But, barring vaporization, I will live peacefully in Providence until the time comes. Anyway, putting up flaky posters in strange cities with unfriendly policemen and vigilantes is hardly the stuff epics are made of."

"We aren't just putting up posters. I haven't told the others this yet, they will figure it out in good time, but Christ really is a vampire. And we have no choice but to kill him."

"If you meet the Buddha upon the road, kill him," said Blue.

"Despite the illusory nature of Buddhism, we would try to enlist him. We have few advantages."

"You are fucking crazy Jack. It's one thing to have some fun, its another to believe in vampires. Christ mother-fucking Mary, you white people got no sense."

"It's true, and you are a known associate of mine, and in pretty serious danger. Not from spiritual seduction, at least I think not, but from the Knights and various other Christian minions. Maybe they will just watch you for a while, and if you are quiet about it, they won't go any further."

"Hi dee hi dee hi," swore Blue.

Rap could see what Jack was getting at. It didn't matter whether there was a Christ the Vampire or not; people would kill for Christ and Christianity, and he had gotten himself ensnarled. The smart thing to do was to just leave town; he wasn't in so deep that he would be followed.

Looking at Jack he knew the man was not trying to scare him or badger him into joining the adventure. Jack was devious enough to be honest when it was appropriate. The question was, was this a good gang? He knew if it were a poor man's army he would have joined in a second. But there was no poor man's army, not in the USA, just poor people's music and myth.

"Christ really is a vampire, Rap."

This statement shook Rap out of his reverie. He knew his mind.

"I'll find out for myself," Rap said.

Marion and Cinder arrived at the Professor's apartment together. They immediately began unpacking the food that Joey and Digger had packed and commenced to consume it. Each had brought a large duffle bag of "essential" clothing. Between them they had $32.57 to contribute to the cause, not including Cinder's mother's Shell Oil credit card. Their presence immediately cheered up the men, who began calculating, subconsciously, the probability of getting into their prospective pants. In a nice manner, of course, fully respectful of their humanity.

The Professor came out, looked at the four freaks, shook his head, and went back into his bedroom. Digger followed him in.

"Time's a wasting, Professor," he advised. "Whether you're going to your parents or coming with us you had better pack up your clothes. Being here after dark is stupid. You aren't stupid."

"Damn straight I'm not stupid!" screamed the Professor. "I don't need this. I don't need you, or Jack, or the bloody asshole Christians. I don't need my bloody parents. I am going to the bank to get my money, then I'm going to pack and go to the airport. Then I'm going to start my life over in another place and I am going to keep my mouth shut."

When he was out the door they found an acceptable album from among his ancient collection of 60's music and put it on at nearly full volume. Thus when Johnny entered she was unable to explain that she had just escaped from her parents by setting fire to her house. She started trying on the other women's clothes, as she had brought very little herself. Meanwhile Joey and Digger were collecting items they thought might prove useful on a trip: tools, blankets, some kitchen ware, and etc.

Jack and Blue came in, turned down the music, and helped the women to re-pack. That done, Jack decided it was time for a speech.

"I think you know this can be a fun trip, but if that's what it is going to be you're going to have to keep your sense of humor. There will be times when the food will be good because you will be half starved, and when lying down on a hard floor will seem like heaven because you are dying to sleep. This is a lively bunch and most of the living will like you and most of the dead will hate you. We have to rid this world of Christ the Vampire, but first we have to get out of Providence. We are going to the bus station, and taking the bus together to Kingston where a friend will meet us with a van."

"Wouldn't it be easier to have the van come here? We aren't exactly overwhelmed with money" said Joey.

"I don't want our enemies to see the van. If they want to drive down to Kingston, then we are out of luck, but I doubt that they will bother."

"The Professor isn't coming with us" said Cinder.

"He's his own man" said Jack.

Just then the Professor came back in from outside, obviously ready to throw a fit. "I can't get my money out of the bank," he screamed, throwing his arms up into the air. "And this bloody chevy followed me along the street."

"So what are you going to do?" asked Digger.

"Those motherfuckers are going to regret they ever crawled out of their stinking graves," said the Professor.

"Right," said Blue.

"Stuff some clothes in your backpack, we have a bus to catch."

The bus station was an easy walk. As far as Jack could tell no one got on the bus to keep track of them. Just before they got to the Cranston station he informed them of the change in plan: they were really being picked up there.

Libby turned on the ignition when she saw the bus pull into the station. In a minute they were packed in and heading for the Connecticut border. Everyone was pleased at the ruse: if anyone were waiting for them in Kingston, by the time the bus got there their van would be across the state line.

By that time the sun had set.

Chapter 6

NIGHT

Hadley had always had things to be proud of, but nothing had ever made a group of Hadley's citizens as proud as the Thomas the Doubter Batbit Church of Hadley. Squeezed inside a mushroom of self-righteousness, members' heads were held high in the clouds of the television cameras beaming their most Christian torsos high above their sleeping asses to less fortunate if perhaps more fanatical followers scattered in front of TV's across the nation. Of course a number of them had not meant to be Batbits in the first place, but had suffered the accident of being born to Batbit parents. Some had been converted back before Reverend Fowler had arrived, and many more had not gotten the bite, you might say, until being lured into the church by the television cameras.

It had been different before Fowler's arrival. The town had been sleepier, more proud of its traditions than of its moral uprightness. It had as much suffered as hosted the presence of Frosty Bacon Women's College. Of course the tourists would go see Colonel McCartney's statue and examples of pre-civil war architecture, but they were generally not particularly impressed by the role of the Fourth Virginia Irregulars in the Civil War, even though almost all of Hadley's people were descendants of those brave warriors. But then not many tourists came to Hadley, if you excepted the shoppers and curiosity seekers from the towns and farms of the foothills leading up to the Alleghenies.

The arrival of a van of young people, including one black male and one black female, was noted by quite a number of people on one fine spring Thursday. The gas station attendant who took their gas money mostly noticed that the women were his age and on the road and did not dress like the local girls. The gas meter readers and electric meter readers and postal workers and farmers in town on business who made up the mid-morning clientele at the easternmost Benny's in Hadley, which was also the closest to the Main Highway, noted their entrance. The ones who were close enough noted that they were clean cut and nice, but yankees and probably students because if they were bums they would not have eaten at Benny's and yet they managed to spend no more than three dollars fifty cents apiece on the meal. The waitress, Mildred, liked them but could not figure out which boys were with which girls. She asked them direct if they were going to Hadley or if they were just passing through.

"We're on our way to Florida State in Tallahassee, Miss, but we wanted to stop in to see the Reverend Fowler's church. Me and Amy here watch his TV show sometimes. Isn't that right, Amy?"

"I don't like to get up so early, though, not on a Sunday," said Johnny, who was temporarily Amy.

"Well, the TV show isn't until Sunday, I guess you know."

"Do you go to his church?" inquired Amy.

"There are lot's of churches in town, miss. Not everyone has to be on TV," said the waitress, with what might have been a note of irritation, but certainly not of envy.

Hadley was large enough to be called a city, but in many ways it operated as a small town. There was a cohesiveness to its people that only a couple of centuries of intermarriage and reasonably stable employment could provide to a small city. True, the best and brightest, or at least the most ambitious sons and daughters, matriculated to Richmond or Washington, D.C. and at times when a factory closed some of the workers would move elsewhere. True, many blacks migrated to the north when there was work waiting there, but mainly people tended to stay in Hadley's familiar circles, comfortable or uncomfortable.

When new people arrived in town they were noticed quickly enough. Those who came by invitation — to take a job or live with relatives, or students — were announced long in advance. Those who came as tourists seldom stayed the night, but when they did they stayed in one of the hotels or motels on one of the major roads into town. Sales men often stayed at the red brick Hotel Stoker downtown, a tradition that dated back to the time they came in by train. Country people came into shop and the men sometimes had a drink at the James River Bar.

Drifters were another matter. The policemen who patrolled downtown knew the regular, town-bred alkies and refuseniks and sharks, and if they somehow missed a man or woman there were only a few bars and coffee shops, one boarding house and one rooming house downtown. The bartenders had, from long experience, learned to distinguish a dangerous man from an alkie from a loser from an honest working man down on this luck. They might pass the word along to the police, who might just keep watch on a man, who might put him up for a night in the county jail, and might escort him to the country line. Sometimes a lucky man would get a tip from a bartender or a fellow drinker about a job. With a bit more luck he would learn of one of the rooming houses up the hill that were less expensive and more pleasant than the one on Main Street.

Sometimes ordinary people entered town by an unusual route or unusual people entered town by the usual route and Hadley's immune system would respond in more complex ways. By the time the Professor and crew, now referring to their collective selves as Dr. Seward, had eaten breakfast three people had asked Mildred what the strange kids had to say for themselves, several more had overheard bits of the conversation, and all were thinking about how they would tell the tale to their friends. Bill Harris, a gas meter reader related to the Harrises of better fortune, a secret agnostic though he was known to sometimes attend Episcopal services with his wife, noted that the group was strongly individualistic: they did not dress like each other and did not talk like each other. From this he concluded that either they had not been together long or that they were together for some purpose: conspirators. He did not believe they were Christians, and he deducted that they had no good in mind for Mr. Fowler. He called up two of his lodge brothers and told them about the kids, asking them to keep a watch out for them and help them if they seemed to need it. From them, by the time the town slept that evening, more than a dozen members of his secret society were on the lookout for Dr. Seward, and several had already spotted them.

Lionel Cabell, owner of the Guaranteed Hardware Store, noticed little about the group except that it consisted of men and women, including a black man and a black woman, and that they were yankees. Lionel was a klan member and his wife a member of the United Daughters of the Confederacy. Usually he did not eat at Benny's, but he was having a late breakfast with a salesman. He knew that Benny's would serve N------, but seldom did, so he was offended that these people had come in. He was a moderate within the klan: he did not believe in lynching N------- unless they had raped a white woman or murdered a white man and were otherwise going to get away with it. He believed in discouraging N------- from moving into his neighborhood, and thus far not only they but most people who weren't racists themselves had been so discouraged. He told several of his friends about the group later in the day, making jokes about the N------- loving white girls having N------- babies, but otherwise took no action.

The face above the prematurely withered body, the one that looked like an aged unhappy lynx, belonged to Virginia Roller, who was also not a regular at Benny's. She did not approve of public places other than Churches, but was taken there by her cousin Jenny, prior to going shopping. She did not approve of Jenny, who was not a Southern Batbit, nor of unnecessary shopping, even if it were supposed to be to look for gifts for a shower. Virginia was married to Thomas Roller, whose brother was Reverend Roller of the Church Street Batbit Church. Virginia could see that Dr. Seward was the spawn of the Devil as soon as they walked in. In particular Jack had the ways of a tempter: pride and hiding it beneath a saintly veneer. The girls were fallen harlots, hardly even aware of the tabernacles that should have been their bodies. Their very clothing and manners were an affront to God. And when George Simon, who had been sitting near their table, told her that the women wanted to see Reverend Fowler, well she knew they were liars and up to no good.

Virginia could not do much about it right away, though she let some of her thoughts be known to Cousin Jenny, who did not agree with them but pretended to in order to keep the peace. As soon as Virginia was home she called Reverend Roller and then Missy Forsberg, who was an important member of Thomas the Doubter Batbit Church, and then a dozen other ladies of various ages who were against abortion, communism, drugs, sex, youth, flirting, pleasure, dirt, foreigners, tobacco, booze and homosexuality.

The Reverend Fowler was much too busy a man to be bothered with such a thing, but various important people in the church were informed by Missy Forsberg and the word went out broadly around Hadley to watch out for Dr. Seward. Among those informed were the Chief of Police and one of his deputies, Barney Nosegay, who was a member of the secret Army of God. Most of those informed, upon hearing that the information came from Virginia Roller, were inclined, if not towards skepticism, towards a wait and see attitude. Not all northerners were personal agents of the devil, the FBI, liberalism and other malignant forces. Also, they knew the business establishment liked Hadley to be seen as a sort of progressive place, the kind of place you could bring a computer factory to. They did not look kindly upon any incidents that would hurt that reputation. The businessmen were glad, however, for the enormous inflow of money to the town economy from Reverend Fowler's operations.

One of those informed of the intrusion of Dr. Seward was Garland Burkholder, who acted as a sort of liaison between the town establishment, descendants of the old aristocracy and manufacturers, and sections of the middle class that had grouped around Reverend Fowler. He did not think it important, but did include it in a note to Colonel Warwick, who liked to keep up on such things. Now Colonel Warwick was a public Episcopalian and was really a Freemason and hence an atheist, but he was friends with Bishop Majorem of the Catholic Church. The Bishop had told the Colonel about possible troubles they were expecting with an anti-Christian campaign led by anarchists. The Colonel decided to put out his own scouts to watch Dr. Seward. He was not adverse to the idea of a campaign against Christianity, which he thought was keeping America backward, but he had no intention of tolerating Anarchy.

After leaving Benny's, Dr. Seward drove first to Frosty Bacon Women's College. They expected there to be a commercialized street running along the campus boundary to meet the needs of the students, but there was none. As was their way, after being squeezed together in the van, they fanned out in groups of two, excepting that the Professor, Johnny and Libby formed a threesome.

When allotted time had expired they began to gather on the great lawn and eat lunch.

"There, but for the grace of capitalist economics, goes I," said Libby, to start things off.

"Yeah, it makes Brown look like a lustbed of rebellion."

"I didn't even see anyone who looked as if they listen to Cindy Lauper, much less punk."

"Some of them probably do, but they keep the records hidden in classical albums and only listen to them late at night, using headphones."

"Can you believe what that girl said? 'If you mean avant-guard, there are some foolish women here.'"

"Where?"

"In the art-cloister no doubt."

"Cubism rearing its ugly head in the eighties."

"And now," said the Professor in a poor imitation of an upper-class southern drawl, "we will take up an important event in the history of our nation, the War in Vietnam. Unfortunately, the semester will be over in fifteen minutes, so our examination will be in the nature of an overview."

To everyone's surprise, when Digger and Cinder returned they brought a woman with them.

"Hi everyone, this is Mary Kate. Let's see, that's Libby and the Professor, Jack, Johnny, Marion, Joey, and Rap."

"Hi everyone."

"Glad to meet you. We thought the campus was dead, based on unscientific sampling."

"Oh, you're right," said Mary Kate, "I'm transferring to Florida State at the end of the semester. Sometimes live people come here, but they usually transfer or are strangled pretty quickly."

"So is anything happening in Hadley? Any signs of rebellion, intelligence, surrealism or humor?"

"I don't know. It's not like there isn't partying here, beer and even some drugs, but it's like fate, born to rich Southerners. Hadley College is better, there's more partying and irreverence, but it's kind of narrow-minded anyway. Real chauvinist too. I heard there were some punks there a few years ago, but they caught a lot of abuse."

"Any sign of vampires, Mary?" This from Jack.

Mary looked confused.

"We failed to explain the true purpose of putting nine people in the van Calcutta and trucking down to Hadley, among other places," said Cinder. "In Providence, Rhode Island it was discovered that Christianity is a vampire cult. In trying to free some young people from the influences of the undead eternal Christ we suffered grave persecution and physical attacks. We decided to engage in urban guerilla cultural warfare. We suspect, because of the presence of Reverend Fowler here, that this may be a center of vampire infestation. We intend to do some actions here."

Mary stared at her for a few moments, then looked at the others, who either smiled back or nodded their heads. "Let's see. Jesus is a vampire because he rose from the dead and people follow him and want to live forever." She smiled. "I don't suppose these vampires drink blood?"

"No, but they sure like to get into wars with heathens."

"That's pretty rich. I know some people who will love it. But I can see why people would be attacking you too."

"Would you like to help?"

"I don't know what I could do."

"Start be telling us what you know about Christians in Hadley."

"Nothing really. I don't even go to Church. I don't imagine it's any worse here than where I grew up."

"This," said Jack, "is obviously a problem we will continue to run into. Sympathizers will know little about the enemy camp, unless their parents are in it. But I'll bet Mary Kate can introduce our two young Christian ladies to someone who can tell them where they can take part it bible study while they are here."

"That would be so kind of you Mary," said Marion, "because, well I do carry a bible, but I still feel I need some guidance and the company of fellow Christians is beloved to God."

Everyone laughed.

"The lOrd AwakInned, and then hE ROSe, and BeinK thIRSty, soUgHt him drINk." (Cornmuffins, 1:23)

"Christ be damned." (Thomas the Doubter, refusing eternal life.)

"I am the resurrection and the life, he who bleeds in Me shall live even if he dies." (John 11:25)

The Reverend Sitwell was a mere 32 years old. He knew he was up to be made the following year, which would be a rare privilege for one so young. Yet he had proven himself many times over. He was worthy of eternal life by virtue of service, of purity, of knowledge and grace. He was thin as a ascetic should be, and his long beard gave him the dignity that some men must suffer age for. His eyes were flames of the Holy Spirit, and his penis had not been smoothed by his hand or greased by the ointment of woman since he was 19 years old. He dressed simply, in black, and was never without his Bible.

"Today's lesson," he began, "is the authority of our prince and master Jesus Christ. His authority is the ultimate authority, to which all other Christian authority is a supplement. His authority is greater even than that of the Bible, greater than that of the Ministry. His authority is the authority of God the Creator, who has given Him authority over man. His authority is eternal and living, for he lives, body and soul, from the time of his birth to the end of eternity."

"Does not the good book say . . ." He swept on and on.

"Yet the world is troubled today, troubled by sin, by war, by the horrors of abortion, by faithlessness, communism, false faith, drugs, adultery. The vast majority of people who live today will die only to be cast into hell. They will not know Christ, they will not be blessed with eternal life. Why? Why do we not live in paradise?"

"The answer is free will, God's blessing and God's curse upon us. If we were mere robots, puppets of God on strings, where would be the merit in serving him? So God has withdrawn from the world, and his two sons, Lucifer and Jesus, battle through the centuries, one to destroy man, the other to aid him. There too is the grace of accepting the living authority of Jesus Christ: it is accepted freely. To follow Christ because someone is pointing a gun at your head or paying you is false and useless. Christ may appear to you, but you must invite him in across the threshold."

"Thus Communism is the greatest work and greatest evil of Lucifer. For the people cannot hear the word of our Lord, and learn the lie that there is no spiritual world, and there is no life after death."

Marion and Johnny struggled to look suitably impressed. It was easier for Johnny, who had more recent practice in looking pious. It was Johnny, too, who had gotten them this far, by quoting bits of the Bible at appropriate points.

The discussion was even more tedious, as various of the students tried to prove their mastery of the Bible by quoting it. Marion and Johnny held up their end by asking questions.

Afterwards, by waiting long enough, they were able to have a word with Reverend Sitwell.

"Reverend, is it possible for Christians to live in the body as well as the soul, I mean, like Christ, living past the normal span of life?"

The Reverend tried to look into Marion's soul, and not being able to, convinced himself that here was someone who might be admitted to the inner secret, or, failing that, serve as a source of life for those who needed it. But since he was not yet made himself it was a matter that would have to be taken up with his own master.

"Eternal life in Christ is not something you should seek out of greed. To be in unity with Christ is to attain a state few people can imagine. Remember the disciples committed miracles, for they were one with Christ. The dead were raised and the sick healed: and why could not such a person live like Christ in the body as well as the soul?"

"How could we learn more about this?" said Johnny.

"It is something that will be for you to hear when you are ready to hear, my child. The important thing for now is to take your Bible to heart and learn to love Jesus."

They managed to escape from the girl Mary Kate had introduced them to and went to look for their friends.

"I'm beginning to wonder if there might not really be vampires. Can you believe Sitwell's answer to your question? He sure didn't say no."

"And I'm sure not going back there."

They walked on a street parallel to the river, Court Street, and almost every intersection had a church. Some were built of yellow or grey limestone, some were of red brick. They were glad that Thomas the Doubter Church was far away, in the middle class white suburbs. They turned away from the river, walking into a black residential district, and were soon at the boarding house that Rap had conjured up for their stay. But the others were not there.

They returned only after they had made a general survey of Hadley with graffiti in mind. "It's too bad we can't do Egality Bible College," grumbled Joey.

"Suicide squads aren't necessary at this point."

"We have serious news for you. This town is more dangerous than you think. We were in a Bible class with a Reverend Sitwell, and we asked him about eternal life, and he basically said it was possible and just keep studying the Bible."

"Holy shit."

"He didn't try and hypnotize you, did he?"

"No, and he didn't try to see us alone or anything. He's a young guy too, kind of creepy, like ice cold unsexual and burning hot mind at the same time."

"But boring."

"Is he connected with Thomas the Doubter?"

"No, he's with First Batbit, downtown."

"OK, we might as well do as we planned," said Jack, "only we'll split before dawn. We can go camping for a few days and let things simmer, then come back and see if anything is more out in the open. It's not like we can go around hunting vampires, all we can do at this point is to wake people up."

And after much discussion about details, it was so agreed.

Owen Diggs should have been dead decades earlier. He had, to keep up appearances, gone west for some forty years and returned as his own grandson. Even so, he was believed to be about sixty years old. He required, to continue life, the life of a child about once a year.

Reverend Sitwell was comfortable in his presence; the man was like a father to him. The room they sat in was an ordinary study lit by sun suffusing through a window and by electric light with books lining the walls, an antique wood desk and a large, out of date globe in one corner. It was with some pleasure that the Reverend told Owen of the two new women in the Bible class and their interest in eternal life.

"That's fine, but the least of our worries right now," said Owen. "Nobody is going to be made anytime soon, anyway. It is not a good time for it." He noted the disappointment on Sitwell's face with pleasure.

"There is a serious shortage of souls available to be sacrificed right now. This missing children thing has hurt us, of course, but mainly there are two problems. One is that too many people have been made, and the deaths that used to occur among us are infrequent now that we have antibiotics and vaccines. The other is the availability of abortion and birth control. Unwanted children are simply not plentiful enough. The Army of God has taken a step in the right direction, but we've been asked to step up the campaign. That means you'll have to do better at recruiting. I suggest you go on a national tour. If you have any problems talk to me about them. Also, we can't always stop the FBI from investigating. So people should be more professional."

"You know the problem there, Owen: professionals aren't easy to recruit."

"That is why you must train them. On this sheet of paper are two contacts who can help with the technical acts of training. You should see to it that their hearts are pure before you turn them loose on your recruits."

"Yes."

"And there is an immediate problem. We have in town a group of people who are propagandizing the Dark Secret. Officer Nosegay should be able to put you on their track. The Catholics in Rhode Island gave them a warning, and instead of listening they have chosen to come causing trouble here. Have one of them killed. Make it clear it is not an accident. I'll leave to you which member of your army is most up to the task. Whoever it is should work alone, no one should know of this but the two of you. There will be an investigation, of course, and since these people are from out of state there might be some screaming and, well, in short, it should be done professionally. We don't know how long they will be in town, so get on it right away."

Owen was glad when the Reverend departed. He closed the curtains, dimmed the lights, and took out the special contact lenses that protected his eyes from bright light.

A number of people, all parked in cars, were watching the rooming house on 8th Avenue that night. Since they were all white and it was a black neighborhood the residents figured it for a stakeout, probably for a drug bust, and Dr. Seward was aware of this too. Nevertheless shortly before midnight they loaded into the van.

Plainclothesman Fife had been ordered to watch the strangers, intervene if they were harassed, and bust them if they did anything illegal. He was there largely due to Colonel Warwick's influence. Parked three cars behind him were four Klansmen, good Christians all, who simply wanted an opportunity to do some N------ and N------ lover bashing. They had been told their victims were communist organizers. Four young bulls from Egality Bible College were parked well past the van in the direction it was pointed. They had been told to simply follow Dr. Seward and attack only if Churches were desecrated, in which case they were to take prisoners and call the police. Policeman Nosegay and a partner were there, unofficially, to make sure nothing went wrong and to cover for Dickson.

Dickson's father had died in Vietnam fighting communism. Dickson had served time in the army and then joined the ministry of Reverend Sitwell and then the Army of God. He was not from Hadley, he had come in that day at Sitwell's request. He was twenty two years old and had already had a hand in bombing two abortion clinics. He was looking forward to killing one of the devil worshipers.

Dr. Seward pulled out in a U-turn and thus immediately shook the kids from Egality Bible College. They also spotted the Klansmen and Nosegay doing their turns. They did not notice Plainclothesman Fife because he did not start right away: he turned on the direction finder to the beeper he had placed on the van. Dr. Seward headed north, then back south, and had soon eluded everyone but Fife.

The Klansmen called a friend and within half an hour half a dozen Klan mobiles were looking for the van, and another sat near Thomas the Doubter Church, which was the presumed target.

Back downtown the Professor, Digger, Rapmaster, Libby and Joey were dropped off. The van continued to the fashionable area near Frosty Bacon Women's College. Jack, Johnny, Marion and Cinder abandoned it. Ten blocks away they quickly stole the license plates off two cars. They put the first set on the second car and took the second set with them. For a while they wandered looking for a car with an unlocked door. When they found it they switched the license plates and Jack hot wired it. They drove back north to do their designated spray painting. Fife knew the van was abandoned, but figured they were in that area and roamed around it looking for them.

The downtown team's plan was to chill for a while to make sure they weren't being followed, then to do some smaller work in dark areas where it likely as not would not be noticed until the morning, and then do two or three churches before escaping back to the hotel. Joey was the only experienced painter among them, so he took charge and was to do the actual spraying himself, with the others to serve as lookouts. They had agreed that if anything went wrong they would meet at the courthouse, and no one would go alone, even if that meant two of them would have to take a bust.

They started close to the river near the bridge. An alley went in off the street; the wall close to the sidewalk would be visible in the day. The Professor stood near Joey while Rap went to one corner with Libby; Digger stood watch at the opposite end of the block. For good measure Joey did both walls; it took him less than two minutes, though it seemed like forever to the others.

The city was dead, which suited them fine. Noise and headlights announced the occasional car, allowing them to duck into alleys or entryways to buildings. After they did a few alleys they walked a dozen or so blocks to the east, where there was a large wall, part of a warehouse, on a street with a dead end by a vacant lot. Joey did a big "Christ the Vampire Wants You for Communion." This took the better part of five minutes and made the crew nervous again. They walked two blocks up the hill and then walked all the way back west, passing one young black man and two winos along the way.

It was past three now, time to hit the churches on Court Street. It was not that dangerous, Joey assured them. The churches were far enough off the street that it was unlikely the sprayer would be spotted, he said. So they started with a church that was of red brick with a high white steeple. Joey waited as two different cars cruised by. Then he sprayed "Christ the Vampire welcomes you!"

"I sure hope these people aren't so stupid they can't figure out this Christ the Vampire thing," said the Professor.

They moved on down the street. As Joey was about to start on some nice yellow limestone Digger whistled and crossed the street.

"It's a guy," said the Professor.

A set of headlights also moved towards them, cruised by. "That was the same car, with four white men in it checking us out," said Rap to Libby. "We had better give the signal to split."

The man walked by, glancing at Joey and the Professor, smiling. Joey began to spray, but before the man got to Rap and Libby he started walking back.

Joey and the Professor walked towards him together; Digger was walking parallel, across the street. The man stopped a body's length from Joey. "Taste God's Justice" he said, pulling a knife with a six inch blade.

He lunged at Joey and into a cloud of spraypaint. Blinded and choking, his cursing was mingled with Joey's cry of pain from being cut. Before Dickson had recovered Digger gave him a solid kick to the head, then grabbed his two friends and said "Let's go!"

A half block away the white Ford that had passed twice screeched to a halt between Rap and Libby and the others. They turned and ran downhill even as men armed with baseball bats jumped out of the car.

Digger said "shit" and turned back away from the Klansmen only to face a enraged, half blinded maniac. He ran across the street and towards the far corner, his friends a step behind, and did not even glance back until they were a block away. The Assassin was stumbling after them. They turned at each corner and soon he was out of sight, and then Joey fainted as headlights appeared in front of them. They dragged Joey onto a lawn and lay down before the car got to them.

Meanwhile Rap and Libby broke left onto Main Street and then started running up the hill at 5th. The Klan lagged back, but then the car picked them up again. In two seconds it was on them and Rap was looking for something to fight with.

Libby was kneeling and firing. The car ground noisily to a halt. She jumped up and they were running again. There was gunfire from behind them, but it went wide.

They did not slow down until they were over the hill and into their black neighborhood. "What was that, anyway?" demanded Rap.

"Thirty-eight" said Libby.

"Pretty handy." He was pissed because the had been holding out on him. "I guess we can forget meeting at the courthouse."

"We should go back to our room if the coast looks clear. If Joey doesn't show up with the others we can go looking for them when the van gets back."

Digger and the Professor dragged Joey further from the street and looked at him. His left arm was gashed just below the elbow and was still bleeding badly. The Professor took his own shirt and used it to put pressure on the wound. He worried that the people in the house might wake up and call the police. It was at least a dozen blocks back to the rooming house.

"Either we carry him or one of us goes to get help or we wait here until dawn or we knock on these people's door and call an ambulance."

"He stopped bleeding and his pulse is OK and I don't trust the ambulance people, for all we know that guy was a pig."

"We haven't seen a cop car."

"If you were declaring open season on vampire haters you might keep the pigs out of the area."

"One of us has to go. You'd better stay here, Professor, I'm more used to moving through the streets without being seen."

Digger moved cautiously, hugging the shadows. It did not take him long to get near the rooming house. He realized now that they should have chosen a back up gathering site in case something like this happened. He became super cautious before he even got near the street. He peered down it from the darkness of a shade tree a block and a half away. He could see no one in cars, but then he could see little of anything. He crept forward, stopping frequently.

When he was three houses away from the house he was forced to conclude that no one was watching it from the street.

His back was slammed against a wall and his arms pinned against it. "What do you think you are doing here, white boy?"

Two black men faced him in addition to the ones that had him pinned. He could think of no lie that would save him. "I'm staying at that rooming house right there."

"Is that right? You one of the nigger-lovers the Klan was here to scalp."

Digger had to make a physical effort to say "I guess. They caught us downtown."

"You let that man be," said the voice of Libby, who already had her .38 out and pointing in their general direction.

"Sure," said the man who had been interrogating Digger, suddenly polite. "We were just looking out for you. There were some Klansmen here earlier, we got in a ruckus with them, so we've been standing watch."

"Thanks, they caught us downtown but I slowed them down some. We really appreciate. Where's Joey and Richard?"

"That man stabbed Joey and we were trying to get back here and he fainted."

"I have a car, miss, if you want we can go pick them up."

Soon they had rousted a black doctor who sewed Joey up and gave him antibiotics.

The people in the van returned unscathed. They all rested briefly, then loaded up and headed out of town as soon as there was traffic.

Chapter 7

THE COUNCIL

They could have met using telecommunications, but few were willing to give up either the ability to influence others through their personal magnetism or the possibility of recognizing the schemes behind the words of their rivals by the added clues of three-dimensionality, smell, and telepathic pickup. They met in the ancient meeting hall beneath the city of Istanbul, and all arrived on time, as was the tradition.

It was a large place for thirteen people to meet, roughly an oval 24 meters across and 60 meters in length with a 8 meter high ceiling. The sacrificial font, white marble contrasting to the red marble walls, sat unadorned in the center. Around it were the couches for the attendees, ancient ironwood crafted with images human and inhuman, with pillows of ancient silk enclosing the most comfortable synthetic foam available. Some of the couches had trays of food and drink beside them. Once the meeting began, no servant was allowed entry, though a clerk took minutes by listening through a conduit that led to an adjoining room.

Of course for the most part the Primes themselves were not physically present. Most could not or would not be moved. But the connections between them and their representatives were so strong that it could be said there was but one being with two bodies between them. Indeed, each of the Primes was a master of numerous bodies and souls, though some influenced their followers in manners different than the others.

The Chinaman opened the session. He was not Chinese by birth or nationality. He was of medium height and build, with dark wavy hair, brown skin and brown eyes. He looked as if he were in the fourth decade, rather than century of his life; passing him on the streets of Athens or Mexico city one would have

He paused, either to let his last sentence have effect or in order to put his thoughts in order, and then continued: "The worst possibility is that an organization will arise that will seek to purposely thwart our plans. I don't mean a Peace Group or some prol rebels. I mean a group that either seeks to take our place as beneficiaries of the Plan or that can see the Plan and our hand behind it and want something else."

When it became clear that he had finished several hands went up, and he chose Osiris. It was, of course, not the body of Osiris, but a body that had, through constant attuning, become a perfect medium for a creature that was reputedly the most ancient of the vampires.

"There can be no plan but the Plan. We have been through this many times before. People must die, one way or another: there is no avoiding it. Else the world becomes a living hell. The only question is, will they die in such a way that the energies will be harvested and civilization begin again under the leadership of the wise, or will their long struggles go to waste? Suppose some group unknown to us demands to share the harvest. We will do what has always been done: crush them or cut them in. Suppose some group wants to wreck the plan without wishing to benefit themselves. This can be trouble, that is why we have met, but such people are suffering from illusions. Those who are basing their actions on illusions cannot defeat those who are basing their actions on reality. So the question is, what should we do about these people, these clever people. Do they know what they are doing? I think not. It is surprising this has not happened in the past. Perhaps we can turn it to our advantage."

Osiris's last phrase caused Cardinal Vlad's hand to shoot up, but he let it drop immediately when Alexander Hamilton was selected to speak.

"My people are investigating the situation, as I know the Cardinal's are. It's obvious now that this problem

little reason to recognize him. He had begun his car
as a thief before graduating to higher things, and w.
both despised and admired by his peers because he had
risen to such great power so quickly.

"We all know that the problems that brought us here
today would not usually warrant such a gathering. We all
know too that these meetings may become quite frequent
as we approach the final days. We cannot afford to allow
our plans to go astray, not simply because we have
worked centuries at them, but because this is a matter of
life and death for us. We are not the sort that will die
when we have the choice to live. Their blood is our wine.
Let the meeting begin, let us be honest with each other,
that our mutual problems will be resolved."

As was tradition the Chinaman looked for a show of
hands. Only one, that of Aleister Crowley, was raised,
and he gained the floor. "I would like to hear from our
American and Christian colleagues, firsthand, just what
the facts are and how the situation is seen as a danger to
the Plan. From what I know it is a danger to certain
interests rather than the Plan itself or our secret college."

Only Young Morgan raised his hand, and he did not
wait for the formality of Aleister's nod to begin speaking:
"You know the facts, and anyone who doesn't should not
have shown up to waste our collective time. As to
factional interests, that will be revealed as we go on.
How much is the Plan in danger? In a sense not at all.
We are the wisest of the wise, the oldest of the old: we
can correct any deviations. But we cannot ignore them.
This is a major deviation. The most likely result of it
getting out of hand is the war starting early, before
conditions are optimal, and even that is unlikely, because
it is difficult to start a major war against our will. But we
cannot be concerned merely with what is likely and
unlikely. We have seen the merely possible happen often
enough, and know the foolishness of failing to take it
into account."

could have been solved by killing the principals, but I would not have done it at the time. The Cardinal did not know what he was dealing with then. Also, let's face it, there's a lot of talk about vampires these days, and we have done little to discourage it. We've even seen it as beneficial. Someone was going to call Christ a vampire sooner or later. What we did not expect was that this bit of the truth would be turned into a campaign that endangered our control of the population of the planet's most important country. I'm not too worried that anyone is going to take up vampire hunting. Even the people who are spreading this propaganda seem to regard it as fiction. A lot of people hate the Christian fundamentalists or Catholics in the U.S. This is their way of getting back at them. These people went out of their way to take action in Hadley, which anyone who does a minimum of research would know is the headquarters of Reverend Fowler, who has been chosen to be a political voice for anti-abortion and other of our policies."

Cardinal Vlad had his first chance to speak. "As you know on a world wide scale Protestants are marginal in comparison to the members of our Catholic Church, and these fundamentalists are but a fringe. We no longer consider these people to be a serious danger to the Church: we know how to handle them. To a large extent they serve as a buffer against atheism and other ideas that trouble humanity. Protestants don't even have their own representative on this council. In the United States the situation is different. The population there has been difficult to control since day one. We did not investigate these rebels until they brought themselves to our attention; how could we? We took reasonable action. Now we must deal with the problem differently. We can keep this out of the major media, but there are large informal communication networks in the U.S. that we have never been able to destroy. We train people not to think, or at least to think what we want them to think, and this can work against us at times. But we will calm their fears and explain away their rationalizations. In Providence, Rhode Island this disease has already largely run its course. I doubt that we lost any young people that we would not have lost to the drug culture or atheist materialism. The problem is not losing control of the American population, as Alexander has stated. The problem is the existence of a group of people who are at least marginally aware of our existence and have available enough information to piece together what that means. They may very well start hunting vampires, or worse still, find other ways to loosen our grip on the situation. I think our best bet is to infiltrate their groups. We've already done that in Providence, but unfortunately their leaders left before this was done."

The Gnome of Zurich was an ordinary looking Swiss banker. His fellows presumed he was a vampire and the Gnome itself, but since the Gnome was often represented at such councils by different individuals, they could not be sure. Now he spoke. "We talk as if politics and religion make the world go round. We know better. We use money to buy much of what we need: labor, loyalty, machines. To a large extent we have learned over the centuries how to control money rather than having it control us, but our science is far from perfect in that regard. The psychological manipulations that will maximize our ability to harvest under the plan rely on certain presumptions, among them our ability to control the economy. This Christ the Vampire business is more dangerous than you suppose because the fabric of the world is highly interwoven and, at this point, stretched a bit thin. We cannot tolerate a severe world wide depression at this point, and thus we cannot tolerate anything that seriously endangers the American economy. That economy is like a junkie: we have to keep it shot up for another decade. If people panic no amount of creating credit will keep the economy alive. If people start burning churches other people will panic. It could be Spain in 1936 all over again. We cannot risk it. The conscious center of this business must be destroyed or coopted."

All were surprised to see Lord Yama signal that he wished to speak. Like Osiris, his power was largely personal rather than based on control over large numbers of people. A classic vampire with bleached skin and black hair, the Death God always gained attention when he spoke.

"Few people worship me. Why should they? I am not a god. Neither is Jesus Christ, or any of us here. We have merely escaped, for the moment, the wheel of life. We live longer than most men, and may live for the better part of eternity, if our Plan works. But what are we? We are clever and lucky and know a great deal, but what are we? Five centuries ago if I could have I would have destroyed Christ. Now I choose to work with him. But if he becomes a liability, I will suggest that some more worthy entity take his place on this council, just as he would do to me. It cannot be otherwise. We have our friends but we are not friends. Suppose Christ died, suppose these people kill him. Would it matter? Probably not, certainly not in itself. Suppose in five years no one believes in us. Will we die? No. Did Peter the Great die? No, he sits here with us, and runs an empire even larger than when he walked among the living. Everyone dies, but no one wants to be born in a chicken factory to be force fed, feet nailed to the floor, waiting to become a meal for some creature a bit more conscious and much more powerful. Who killed Count Dracula? No one powerful: a mortal clerk and a mortal doctor. Who put an end to Albert? This very council. Where did we come from? Mud and a billion fucks and an infinitude of trials and errors. Today a million people will die and no one can blame us, we did not program their genes. This year a dozen vampires will be made and half a dozen will die. We may not walk out of this council alive: death is always a possibility, even for us. Yes, we take precautions: we have bodies stashed in a dozen places, just as a banker owns stocks in many companies. The Plan is a precaution, not a necessity. I think we should capture a few of these trouble makers: I would like to talk to them. I have few people under my control, but they are skilled: they would not fail us."

The Mullah spoke next. Little was known about his Master, but much was known about his connections with Sufies, sultans and the Iranian Islamic Revolution. "In the old days fruit was not picked until it was ripe. Then people wished to ship it long distances, and they picked it green so that it would ripen in transit. Then they used migrant workers and even machines to pick the fruit, and it became desirable that the fruit on a farm all ripen at the same time, so that the machines or laborers could be moved around efficiently."

He paused and then continued. "In the old days people brought us sacrifices. Then we learned that we could harvest great energy when people were slaughtered in war. Now we are approaching the opportunity to fully transubstantiate ourselves and our servants. We are also approaching the time when we can expand beyond this planet. We are powerful, but we have some weaknesses. One is that we have created a great body of scientists, governments, and armies to do our bidding. This would not matter, but we still depend on material bodies for our existence. If this great force sought to find us and destroy us, they could. They would not get everyone of us, but they would certainly disrupt the Plan. People learning that Jesus Christ is a vampire, one of us, would be of no importance to me if it were not for the possibility of this weakness coming to the fore. What if a vampire were caught and we lost control of the situation? What if one of our followers talked to save his life and were believed? We have a grip of steel, but we have based it on an illusion, Osiris. We have based it on the belief by all but a few men that we do not exist."

Cardinal Vlad spoke again. "All these points are well taken. The situation presents unlikely but serious dangers for the entire Secret College. Obviously it poses great danger to the Christian World even if none of the eventualities that worry some of you come to pass. So I propose that we take strong action against these people, physically destroying them wherever we find them. We can't do this without a major mobilization of Christians in the U.S., and yet we don't want to risk showing our hand. As you know there are numerous other problems with the population of the U.S., and we have contingency plans for dealing with them. I think it is time to crush the democratic forces in the U.S. and bring the scientific community in particular under direct control. We have people in place, within a year we can have an iron grip on the U.S. Then we can prevent a popular movement against us based on this current hysteria."

Half a dozen Council members now wanted the floor. By custom Vlad chose among those who had not had a chance to speak.

Peter the Great was a powerful creature; less cautious than most of his kind, he generally came to such conferences in person. It was he who was responsible for regenerating the Russian State through the Bolshevik coup d'etat and his zombies Lenin, Trotsky and Stalin. He spoke with a thinly veiled edge of contempt in his voice. "The Cardinal is a wise man, as is his master Christ. No other creature has so transcended this material plane, no other creature keeps in such close contact with its minions. I am sure he has thought out the situation carefully and feels his plan is the best of our options. But I am not so sure that hunger should be our guide. Let's face it, Christ has an appetite. He's in control of other people, but not of himself. He was a major impediment to the implementation of many crucial aspects of the Plan. A more authoritarian America, that's less of a big change than having Vlad and his cohorts running it. America is a goose we all have an interest in, particularly me. Perhaps I will get back my Alaska in this bargain? Better still, I think the U.S.

should end its space program. For that I would even throw in a bit of a Red Menace to help out our dear Cardinal."

Now almost everyone wanted to speak, and Aleister Crowley got a turn. "Sometimes I wonder if we are dealing with reality. How many people know of this Christ the Vampire story? How many really care? Do we need to get hysterical every time an anarchist throws a bomb or some new religious cult mushrooms? Does this warrant a coup d'etat in the U.S., with all the unknown variables that entails, including Alaska for Peter and bones for all sorts of petty tyrants and parasites? If the Cardinal wants to take responsibility for killing some fools, that is fine, he does not need my permission or the council's. If he wants help to exterminate these people, I'm willing to consider it. Beyond that he's in for a fight. We've done quite well when we've minimized our meddling with mortals, and I see no reason for straying from that path."

Alexander Hamilton spoke. "I have a keen interest in the governance of the United States, and you all know I have long favored stabilizing more during this final period. However, the situation is fairly well under control, if we can keep this Christ thing quiet. Certainly any U.S. government is going to continue the space program at some level of funding. I would like to take up Lord Yama's offer of help, though not Aleister's. It would be just like Aleister to aid these rebels."

Several people spoke to concur with Alexander, including The Joker. The Chinaman spoke when no one else had raised a hand: "Weishaupt and Simon have not spoken. Do either of you wish to?"

Weishaupt simply concurred with the others. Simon the Magician paused thoughtfully, then spoke slowly and with resonance. "I think science has done its job. True, we need more medical knowledge, and have no general problem with science. But the widespread existence of scientific attitudes can only hurt us between now and the fulfillment of the plan. I am considering putting on a Magic Show. I could use some more minions, and it might be both a blow to popular science and a distraction from the Christian problem. I will let you all know when I make a final decision. As to the immediate matter, I agree it is best to destroy these people, though I cannot help with that myself."

"Does anyone else wish to speak before I offer a summation?" said the Chinaman. No one did.

"It seems that we are in agreement that we will take the means at our disposal to destroy everyone propagating the idea that Christ is a vampire. The main burden of this will fall upon Cardinal Vlad. Let's have a show of hands in favor."

All were in favor of this option. Without a further word each left the chamber.

Chapter 8

BERKELEY

"Woe! Look at that! What kind of coop is it?" asked Cinder.

"Let's go see," said Jack, knowing full well what it was.

Dr. Seward rolled into the parking lot, followed by a yellow Volkswagen bug. Two people who had been in Hadley dropped out: Joey, whose wound had become infected, and Marion, who had stayed with him to take care of him. They had picked up two fellow travellers and their car, Bayou and Rose, who had just escaped from a Christian cult known as The Eternal Way and who wanted to help warn others.

The Coop turned out to be a big supermarket, as large as an A&P or a Safeway. In addition to a regular selection of consumer foods there was a big space filled with barrels containing grains, beans, dried fruit and other items in bulk. The people who were shopping might have been shoppers anywhere in the U.S.: casually dressed women, men in work clothes with or without long hair and beards. Cinder asked and found out that you did not work to belong in this Coop; you bought a share, and then the Coop kept tab of your purchases. If there was a profit at the end of the year you got a refund in proportion to how much food you had bought. "It sure is funny seeing a Coop where you can buy things like meat and white rice and name brand cereal," commented Libby.

Jack guided them to Ho Chi Minh Park to have a picnic and a meeting. They ate first, huddled in the shade of a small tree. Then they talked about various things: the drive, incidents in cities they had visited, articles from a newspaper they had bought. Some, like Cinder and Rapmaster, spoke a lot; others, such as Johnny and the Professor, spoke not at all. When the topic turned to what to do in Berkeley people started raising hands. The person who had spoken last would call on the next person.

Jack spoke first. "We know some people here, and we can raise hell with relative impunity, but our goal was never to just make fun of Christians. We are facing problems that are nationwide, or rather worldwide, in scope. We have some evidence that Jesus is really a vampire, or at least his followers are, and lots of evidence that this idea, whether or not it is true, is frightening to the religious establishment. So there are several paths we can take, and since there are quite a few of us it should be relatively easy to recruit a few more people here in the Bay Area. We should find more effective ways of building anti-vampire groups in different areas of the country, and go back on the offensive against places like Hadley."

Jack called on Cinder. "I think the punks and anarchists should relate to this pretty well. I don't think anyone is going to believe us about Christ really being a vampire, but that isn't what's important. If a lot of people are talking about it, then soon everyone will know and take it for what it's worth. I think the best thing I can do is go back to hanging around with other punks. After all, this is a center for that sort of thing, they even publish 'Maximum Rock & Roll' here."

Jack called on Rose to speak next. She spoke in a soft midwestern drawl: "That's all fine, but I never met a punk before a few days ago. It seems to me like the people we are trying to reach are Christians, especially the ones who are just in churches, the ones who haven't been born again. They don't realize what it is they are supporting. I thing the born-again ones, the ones that are directly under some control from Christ, are too far gone to try to deal with right away. Maybe we could write up something and hand it out and talk to people. I know you think it's dangerous, but I just don't think many people are going to be influenced by punks or anarchists."

Johnny spoke. "We have to look at our resources. It's not like we can take out full page ads in all the local newspapers. And we have to look at what we are up against. If it were really supernatural they would have clobbered us already. But they haven't been able to touch us except in Providence and Hadley. They have enormous control, all those Catholic schools and churches and politicians and all, but they are also spread thin. They'll be pissed as hell when they realize how we are screwing up their system for producing zombies, but they can't exactly take out ads in the papers saying "Contrary to vicious gossip, Christ is not a vampire." I'm not against staying here a while, but our best bet is to keep moving and hitting the towns and cities hard when we can."

Several people raised their hands now, and Libby got the turn. "Those Klansmen, or whoever they were, sure meant business back in Hadley. And Johnny sure is right about the control these people have. Which means they control the police, the FBI, the IRS, and the press, one way or another. We can spraypaint walls and they will sand them down the next day. Some people's eyes will be opened, but I doubt it will be self-perpetuating. The Christian churches have been around for a long time, and have incorporated a lot of popular stuff in order to stay in business. I think we have to build a base here in Berkeley, where it is hard for them to fuck with us, and then send people out to do the kind of thing we've been doing. Also, we ought to publish something explaining about Christ the Vampire at length. That way people will read it and know better how to fight."

Bayou spoke. "All of that is OK, but whatever you believe, I know there are real vampires out there. Maybe they aren't the kind you see in movies, but the reality is worse. This Christ thing can appear to people and do away with their reason, and he has lots of ministers doing his work. Maybe there is a body somewhere. If there is, we have to kill it. Maybe some of the ministers are vampires and Christ is some sort of spirit they conjure up together. In that case the ministers have to be killed, unless we can find some other way to fix them. I'm for telling everyone about this, because people locally will have to deal with the local ministers, but I think we're going to have to take responsibility for going after Christ himself."

Bayou sat there thinking while four people had their hands up. After a few moments Rap reminded him: "Call on someone. Bayou. Yeah, call on someone."

Bayou called on Digger.

"Sounds like everyone is going off in a different direction," said Digger. "That's cool, because there are a lot of directions to go in. But here we are in San Francisco, home of some very astute heads, and we are trying to decide what to do without talking to them. Now I know most Deadheads are going to say "this isn't cool, I'm not a Christian, but Jesus was a good man." And they are right to grove on their various things. They don't realize what a disaster it is when Christians start persecuting heretics and all. But not everyone who's a head will think that. I'll bet some will help. And they will know heads all over the country. More important, they know about weird things, and we are definitely dealing with weirdness here. 'When the going gets weird, the weird turn pro.' So let's talk to some of the other pros."

The Professor had been biding his time; he liked to hear what other people said before he spoke. "I'm not at all convinced that Christ is a vampire, and while I'm sure that I would not want to live anywhere that Christians held political power, I'm not sure this is an immediate danger in the United States. I do think that Christianity screws up people's minds, and it does it to them when they are helpless children. I want to continue the campaign, but I don't want to keep running around the country. I won't stop anyone else from doing that. What

I would like to do is some writing. We could put out a newsletter or something. We could also print up some stickers and posters to sell. Then it's up to the people, as our anarchist friends would say, to take direct action."

In the end they made the decision to use their remaining money to rent a small house. They would get jobs and start talking to people. Then they could do the various projects as resources permitted.

It was Digger who arranged the meeting with Flora at the Blue Streak. If anyone knew Flora's name or occupation before she arrived in the Haight in 1965, they weren't telling. She was just Flora and she needed no Social Security number because the government did not know she existed. She sold medicinal herbs to a small, reliable clientele. She looked about 35 years old, which some people claimed was how old she looked in 1965, and this was responsible for the loyalty of certain customers, though they did not visibly benefit from it.

She did not seem out of place in the restaurant; that would have been difficult. The Blue Streak had a reputation as being illegal, when in fact it was licensed to operate. You had to walk down to an unmarked and unlocked door to get in, and then if you were straight (mentally, not sexually) you would probably walk right back out. There was no problem just dressing straight, lots of people had reason to do that, there just never seemed to be many of them there at the same time. Flora might have gone over and tried to make friends with a new person, which might have been taken wrongly by people unused to women wearing black dresses with necklaces of miniature human skulls.

When introductions with Rap and Cinder were complete Digger started to explain about Christ the Vampire. Flora listened carefully for a while.

At a pause she interjected: "When is a bank not a bank?"

Digger stopped. "I don't know" he said.

"When it's burned."

The three of them looked at Flora. "I don't get it" said Cinder.

"I never did like banks," said Flora. "They end up being more powerful than politicians. Only if you have a beef with a bank not only are you going to lose, because they will just cut off your credit, but you can't even get vengeance with a gun. It doesn't make any sense to shoot the tellers, and if you shoot the president they'll just get another one, and if you shoot the board members they'll elect a new board and their children will thank you for the early inheritance."

"So you have to burn it down."

"Yes, exactly. But that's a bit extreme if you just have a private beef with the bank over a few hundred dollars, don't you think?"

"I guess so," said Digger. "Are you suggesting we should burn all the churches down?"

"It would certainly send their insurance premiums up," said Rap. "Maybe we should burn down the insurance companies, too."

"Do you think Christ is a Vampire?" said Cinder, straight to Flora.

Flora looked her in the eye. "Sure would explain a lot."

"If Christ is a vampire, how should we deal with him?"

"Supposing" said Flora "that a vampire is just a person who somehow lives longer than most, say a lot longer. Well, that person might be a perfectly fine person, might even be a vegetarian. Why should she die or get old just because everyone else does? Suppose there were someone evil, who was a vampire. Thought he was god, or wanted to order people around, or liked to make people suffer. Maybe even schooled in occultism, capable of hypnotizing people from a distance and getting them to do things they would not have thought of themselves.

"So let's not call them vampires, lets call them old ones. Some of the evil old ones bother the good old ones so much that they fight among themselves on occasion. Mostly, however, the old ones have their own projects and keep to themselves. Now, I believe Christ may have indeed risen from the dead. The question is, why did he not appear more to his earlier followers? Maybe he feared he would be killed. Maybe he was even a good vampire, but when he started trying to control people at a distance, they ended up controlling him. Christianity became an organism, so to speak, with both a bureaucracy and feedback between Christ and those in his control. Remember Christianity almost fell apart after the Roman empire did, only the Irish monks saved it from extinction. Well, maybe Jesus got his head together once all the uneducated zombies lost their contacts with him. So he did better the second time around, using less personal contact and more bureaucracy. That would be the late middle ages. But things had changed. Religion was already endangered by the rise of science, which occurred mainly in the Moslem countries, North Africa and the Middle East.

"Old Ones get greedy for life. They get senile too, and have trouble changing. So Christ got to be a worse and worse curse on the world as the centuries passed. You want to get rid of Christ, or at least render him powerless. You could try to find him, but he's probably pretty well hidden. So your only hope is to cut off his supply of food, human beings, and disrupt the hierarchies that keep the food supply coming."

When she had finished Flora laid a dollar bill on her table, which would pay for her tea, stood up, and walked out the door before anyone else could react. When Digger tried to reach her later she was not home, and they later heard she had disappeared.

"Jesus Christ" commented Rap.

"You said it," said Digger.

"Do you think she knew what she was talking about?" said Cinder. The other two just stared at her.

"Do you think she knows some vampires?" said Rap.

"Old Ones," said Digger.

"Hi, can I sit down?" A girl in her early twenties with long brown hair and a tasselled cowboy leather shirt sat down. "Flora doesn't come here often. She gives me herbs to keep the water from burning out my body. That was really cool what she said. I didn't know Christ was a vampire. It must be strange to live for ever. Are you going to hunt for him? If you are I'll go with you. I never finished high school but I know the streets and can keep my nose filled anywhere. Berkeley's getting kind of dull. I'll bet he lives in Jerusalem? Know why? Because there are always wars going on out there and he'd feel at home there. Bet you I could find him in no time. I can see right through people. There was a vampire in here once. I told my friend Sarah that he was a vampire but she said he wasn't because he didn't have fangs and she could see him in the mirror. But what Flora said, that makes sense because the mirror and bats and stuff are just myths. He said he was from Nashville but I didn't believe him. He was old, he should have been dead. Where are you staying? Come on, let's split, no sense in staying here."

"No drugs," said Digger.

"Can't take the risk. People are out to bust us," said Rap.

"No problem. I take them, I don't need them. Shake hands. I'm Penny. What's your name?"

"I'm Digger, and this is Cinder and Rap. I'm not kidding about the drugs. We aren't Puritans. This is a heavy trip. If you come with us you come clean. You're so high on speed your blood could keep a sloth awake for a week. You don't know what you're getting into."

"Oh yeah?" Penny said. She turned to another table and yelled "Hey, Marie, fire sale." Marie came over and Penny sold her a small plastic bag of white powder for $12, which was all the cash Marie had on her.

"You think you're so smart. Well, want to know something? Two nights ago two men were in here looking for your friends. 'We're looking for two guys, one named Jack, the other goes by Professor. They talk about vampires.' That's what they said. Left a number to call, too. They weren't pigs either. I know undercover narcs before they even walk into a room."

"Let's split," said Cinder.

They had rented a three bedroom house in the mainly African-American, run down section of Berkeley west of San Pablo Avenue. Several had already landed jobs, and, living three and four to a room, they expected to have money to start making posters and a newsletter by the end of the month. People, mainly political people, came by to argue with them; they wanted support for their political projects. Most did not want to offend Christians, even though they were atheists.

Jack had no problem recruiting Rain to the cause. Rain had been 17 when she joined the Symbionese Liberation Army after Tania had become its de facto leader, when its main purpose was setting off bombs as the New World Liberation Front. Like many members, she had never been caught and was not named by Tania or any of the other members who were caught by the police. After that she worked as an independent both underground and aboveground, not wanting to join any vanguard parties. She was intent on changing things, and did not want dogmatism or nearsightedness to get in the way. Diplomatic, she had learned to avoid directly criticizing the various leftist parties. As a result she had many friends and few enemies. She was skeptical about Christ being a vampire, but saw the political value of the anti-vampire campaign. She did not believe right-wing Christians were the main political problem in the U.S., or that the ruling class would allow them to take over. They were, however, an important prop for the capitalists, and if that prop were undercut the entire structure might slide to the left. She sent letters out to friends about Christ the Vampire, and also acted as ears in

Berkeley concerning anyone getting nosy about Dr. Seward.

Penny became their main person as far as finding out about vampires from the Berkeley freaks. She did not tell them that she was more interested in eternal life than in killing Christ the Vampire. On the other hand she had no desire to give up her freedom to Christ or anyone else, even if they could offer her a few extra centuries of partying for it. She was sure that Flora's story was basically accurate, and that she might be able to find out from some good old one what the secret to immortality was. She was sure a good old one would show if they put the word out in the proper way.

She introduced the Professor to the Madman of Telegraph Avenue. It was not a proper introduction. Taking the Professor down Telegraph from the university, she led him past the jewelry and t-shirt and new age knick knack tables and the mixture of straight looking students and old and young dayglow types. She knew the story about the Madman: he had been a Professor of Physics at U. Berkeley and flipped out. For years he had stood out on Telegraph Avenue, grey beard and hair growing longer, sometimes mumbling to himself, sometimes carrying on conversations with passersby, real or imagined, sometimes lecturing as to a class. The common denominator was that no one understood what he was saying, though some recognized that at least some of it was about physics. When they approached him he was near Krishna copy, wearing a tattered greying undershirt and a dirty but relatively unworn pair of green pants.

"Then nothing becomes something in green field," he was saying. "The contradiction implies the basis is incorrect, the manifold is incorrect, and the color scheme is uncertain. Pakistan. Densities higher would reduce volatility, but compound error of criticality. Never send Sundays in for Mondays, the effect of such things is in the eye of the beholders. Where's my hat? Where's my belt? Eternity sitting in genetic abreaction. Models of silicate life. If it's incorrect then something is correct, you must start with a new color scheme and presume elasticity. Eliminate that and you know elasticity and inelasticity and the wrong direction, so that isn't the basis of the manifold. Ah hah!"

"Max," said Penny, "this is Professor Holbach."

"If you notice something, and look again, it's your imagination, which is another manifold altogether. If you are looking for something and you find it there's know way of knowing if it was there or if it was created by the process of looking. Am I not correct?"

"Yes," said the Professor, "that's correct."

"Which is not simply Heisenberg. It's the basis of mental homeostasis, which puts us right at the point where we should be, mass and momentum. However, you are interested in other questions. Pakistan again? Perhaps Troy. No way of being certain without better communications. Holograph. Answer back."

"Right again," said the Professor. "We're looking for someone hiding in many minds, commonly called Christ. Can you give us a location?"

"Easy, easy, easy. Easy as pie. So low, you can't get under it. But a more interesting question is . . . no, they are closing in. Up into the sky it went, and then they started closing in. Too early, must wait, can't let them have it. Wish there were someone to tell, but maybe if green does not work blue will. If I were to tell you, would you tell? Up, Up, Up. Pakistan!"

"If you want to tell your secret," said the Professor, "I'll listen, but mainly I want to know about Christ, Jesus Christ, his physical location, a city if you know it."

"They know. They are listening. The secret is safe, but I can tell you this: everywhere must begin somewhere. The place to begin is in Jerusalem. GRT! It's obvious to eyes like mine. They know what the secret is: up, up, up. Upside down, why not, inside out, and up, up, up. But can't tell how. Torture did not work, I'm mad, mad, mad.

Pakistan! Critical density, we're all living on borrowed time. Hurry!"

"Your help is greatly appreciated," said the Professor. "Can we do anything for you in return?"

"Hurry, Hurry, Hurry, they are coming." With that the Madman began to mumble to himself.

"We'd better go," said the Professor.

"What was he saying? Did you understand it? Are we going to go to Jerusalem?"

"He was talking physics talk when we first came up. He thinks he discovered the secret of anti-gravity and that people tortured him because he knows the secret. Who knows, maybe he does, but most physicists think anti-gravity is science fiction. Then again, if he did discover it, I'm sure there are plenty of people who would torture or kill to have that secret. Sure, he thinks that Christ is in Jerusalem, but that was your guess too. He might have read it from you somehow. It's a natural guess for anyone, even someone who is semi-mad. We can't put too much stock in it."

They walked on down Telegraph past the main business section and turned right into a residential area to walk back towards downtown Berkeley. A tan cadillac drove past them and into a parking space in front of them. Two men got out and stood chatting beside the car. Penny eyed them and said "Let's cross the street."

They crossed the street and the men got back in the car. "We're being followed," said Penny. "We've got to lose them before we get back to the house. The BART station is our best bet: they can't follow us in the car, and if they follow on foot it should be no problem losing them. Keep an eye out. If they are serious there will be a team, either another car or someone picking us up on foot."

The car came up right beside them and the men jumped out. "Run!" yelled Penny, but it was too late, other men appeared in front of them and they were quickly pinned and forced into the car. The two of them sat in the middle of the back seat with a man to either side pointing a gun at them.

They were driven over the Berkeley hills into the hot desert and air-conditioned suburbs. The Professor worried because their captors made no attempt to keep them from knowing where they were going: that meant it was unlikely they were meant to be set free. After driving through one of the suburban towns they turned off the road into the brushlands on a dirt road. Eventually they went through a guarded gate and were escorted out of the car into a large ranch style house. Then they sat on a bed in what was obviously a bedroom, with one of their guards watching over them, pistol in hand. After a while another guard came in and tied their hands behind their backs.

Eventually an older man in jeans and a plaid shirt came in, dismissed the guard, and closed the door. He had blond hair and crinkled skin; his nose was beginning to get bulbous. When he spoke it was with the rural drawl common to the interior of California.

"So we have caught the infamous Professor Holbach. And his companion, a drug pusher, Pennelope Smith. It seems you've been doing the devil's work, and there is much to be undone. It's a pretty big desert out here. Two bodies in a deep grave would never be found. And you value your lives, I'm sure. So why don't you just cooperate, and open up your souls to salvation. Why don't we start with a prayer. You remember your prayers, don't you? Let's try the Lord's Prayer."

The man said the prayer without their help.

"Well, we can't force you to pray. But hearing other people pray may help you see the light. Still, we don't have eternity for this project. We want to know some things today. Like where are your friends staying, and who is the contact for the groups in other cities."

"If your men weren't so stupid," said the Professor, "they would have followed us to our friends. Don't you let them watch TV?"

The man did not seem bothered by this remark. "We are not overly adverse to technology, when it suits Christ's purposes. For instance I have with me some sodium Pentothal, which will help you become more cooperative. It's much faster than beating you or starving you."

"You've lost," said the Professor. "We didn't set up the groups in other cities. We just let the people know the truth and they set up their own groups. We don't even know where they are. Your followers are going to drop like flies and then you won't have any money and your whole system will fall apart. You are doomed. Why don't you save yourself by letting us go."

"You are quite mistaken. Your story is but a small problem for us. I understand that you won't cooperate of your free will, but you will cooperate."

A loud crash startled the three of them and a body hurled into the room onto the man. Another man was standing there and their interrogator was lying unconscious on the floor. The door opened but the guard was grabbed by the neck and immediately went limp. The strange man grabbed the Professor and threw him out the window. Then he did the same with Penny. He picked up each of them under an arm and ran into the brush. A few gunshots were fired from the house, but none came close to them.

When they were out of sight of the house he let them down. He talked as he untied their binds: "Sorry about throwing you out the window, but I'm not fast enough to dodge bullets. It will probably be a minute before they start looking for us, what with their leader dead. But we still have to hurry. This way."

They jogged, with the stranger sometimes carrying Penny. Half an hour later they came to a pale blue Volkswagen bug and he loaded them in. Only then did he talk again.

"You have to be more careful. You're doing pretty well, but everyone is looking for you and the people who are putting out the contract only want you alive enough to make sure all of you end up dead. The Madman has been under constant surveillance for a decade. They record everything he says. They weren't using him to get to you, but they sure reacted quickly enough. I'm Eccarius. I'm what you would call a vampire, except that I don't generally kill people and I'm independent. I never went in for the religious stuff, used to be a Marxist back when I was young. Now I'm an anarchist, I have been since Kautsky's times. I'm not that old, less than two centuries, and I intend to live longer. So I'm just going to drop you back in Berkeley and wish you luck. Anyway, there isn't much else I can do for you."

The Professor tried asking Eccarius questions, but the answers were always "I don't know" or "I can't say." Soon they were back in Berkeley and having to tell their story to the others.

"So there really are vampires," said Rap.

"Not necessarily," said Jack. "There are several possibilities. One is that this Eccarius fellow really is as old as he says. By the way, there was an Eccarius who was a pretty important early Marxist, I think he was even a chairman of an early convention of the International. So that would fit. Just as likely he is a strange dude who really did rescue you, and wants you to believe he is a vampire. It's even possible that he was working with the kidnappers, either to make you think there really are vampires or to find out where we are all living."

"I think he was a vampire," said Libby.

"It was certainly a good act," said the Professor.

"Berkeley sure is a strange place," said Rose.

"What was it that Eccarius said about the Madman?" asked Bayou.

"He's under constant surveillance. Maybe someone thinks he really invented anti-gravity."

"And he said something about looking for Christ the Vampire in Jerusalem, right?" said Bayou.

"Something like that. It was more ambiguous. I can't remember his last words."

Someone knocked on the door. They had been so excited about the latest incident that they had failed to establish security. In fact, they had been quite lax about that after they got to Berkeley. Now they were tense as Cinder carefully looked out of a window. "It looks like just one guy. I guess I'll answer it."

When she opened the door the man said "Hi, I'm Dylan. I was told I can find Jack here."

"Dylan? Come on in. How are you? I haven't seen you in years."

"I'm not hard to find. Rain said you need some help on vampires."

"Yes, especially Jesus Christ. We think that he and many of his followers are vampires. Also, we'd like to know if they are material or spiritual. We need facts, not just a rundown on myths and fiction."

"Sure. Of course, a basic human desire is long life. And there is quite a bit of speculation as to what causes aging. We might all be becoming vampires soon if this new drug, aminoguanidine works. As to creatures that have to drink human blood in order to live, I think mosquitoes are the source of that legend. Maybe leaches. And mosquito born diseases cause people to weaken and die."

"So you don't think Christ is a vampire."

"I didn't say that. In fact I think the modern vampire myth is based fairly directly on the life of Jesus as interpreted by pagans who resented the intrusion of Christianity, not to mention the persecution they suffered and the taxes and tithes they had to pay. How much more obvious could you get than say 'Do this in remembrance of me' and then drink blood and eat flesh? And if you drink His blood you become like Him.

"But you probably figured that out for yourselves. You want to know the present status of the cult, aside from its manifestation as the public church. Quite a number of people have written about this, in code of course. Making it public knowledge meant certain death. There were easier ways to fight the Christians, most notably by dividing them and by introducing science and atheism. Whether the rather continuous references to Christ's nature in the literature is because the word was passed from adept to adept and generation to generation, or was sufficiently obvious that people figured it out, or was due to people who were initiated into the cult and somehow escaped, I can't be sure. Probably all three."

There was a pause. "So what did all these people say?"

Dylan resumed. "Christ exists in bodily form and is guarded by people in his complete control, in Rome. He also exists as a diffuse conscious intelligence spread over the minds of many believers. He can appear directly to people when he so desires. Also, people in certain psychological states are susceptible to becoming part of this group mind. Finally, some of those involved also live much longer than normal human beings, and these require the blood of infants, or at least believe they do. According to my deciphering of Albert Magnus, the blood is not drunk, it is transfused in the same manner as modern medical transfusions."

"Thanks, Dylan" said Jack. "Are you still hanging out at the library?"

"I live there, except to sleep. Please don't tell anyone that I told you this. If you want to tell people on your own behalf, that's fine."

"We won't tell anyone we got it from you. I just wanted to know where to find you if we have further questions. I have just one right now: where in Rome does he live?"

"According to Albert Magnus, under the Lateran Cathedral. But he could have moved since then."

"O.K. thanks."

Dylan left and they called a council of war, but for the next day. Jack wanted Rain to be there and to locate another friend first, and the others were agreeable. They also decided that some of the other people they had been talking to would be invited.

Jack had no trouble finding Joe the Pimp; he had merely been putting the task off. Joe was sharing a big condominium with Blue Box, a Yippy expert at using the long distance phone wires for free, and a bodyguard, Thad, a karate expert.

"It's totally surveillance proof," explained Blue Box. "That box there is a decompensator. It uses the entire wall as a speaker element, only all it does is compensate for any noise going on in here. We could play a hundred watt stereo at full blast and you couldn't hear it outside. The entire apartment is also a Faraday box, so no radio waves go out. Of course the phone is tapped, so we don't use it except to order pizza, that sort of thing. We have scramblers, but it's expensive to give descramblers to everyone we know and change all the codes all the time, and the government and phone company can descramble anything if they really want to."

"What about lasers?" said Jack.

"What about them?" said Blue Box.

"All you'd have to do is aim in a laser through the window and read its reflection off any object in the room. The object would pick up the sound waves, and . . ."

"Yipes!" said Blue Box. "I hadn't thought of that! Don't tell Joe, he'll be pissed. Shit! What am I going to do?"

"Buy yourself a laser and start spying."

"Right. Did you think of this? Maybe no one is doing it yet. No, it's obvious. If you thought of it someone else did. First I've got to get this place secure again. I'll have to put some kind of coating on the window."

Jack was glad to get away from Blue Box and talk to Joe. Joe had started as a real pimp running girls on San Pablo Avenue in Oakland. He saw that was a losing game and joined the Black Panthers, set up a call girl string, and managed to go to college. The police busted up his strings as often as they could: they didn't like the Panthers. Joe got better at it each time, and began learning about the girls' clients. By the time he had his college degree he was training the girls to pump their clients for information. Sometimes he was able to sell the information to his client's business competitors. It was safer and more lucrative than blackmail. When the Panthers fell apart he supported any project he thought would undermine the system, ranging from radical bookstores to research projects.

"So Jack, what's happening? I heard you've got yourself into some heavy shit."

"Just having fun. You know me. I figured you would have heard, and I hope you can tell me from where. What are we up against at this point?"

"Christians and freelancers. The governments aren't involved, though that could be because you're in Berkeley, my guess is it would be different elsewhere. The Christians can mobilize a lot of people, and they can be vicious, but they aren't too smart. I'd watch your place pretty carefully, they're going over Berkeley block by block. After that they'll either try to pick off your people one by one or do a frontal assault on your house."

"We can handle them. Lot's more people in Berkeley will be looking out for us than helping them. What about the Freelancers?"

"You know how hard it is to prevent an assassination."

"Is that what it's down to?"

"Well, you know me. I've let it be known that anyone who touches a hair on your chiny chin chin is history. But some people will take the risk. Right now they only have pictures of, lets see" he picked up a sheet of paper "you, a Rick Holbach, known as the Professor, and Libby Washington identified, plus some other pictures, here they are, of your friends."

The pictures were all of them outside the boarding house in Hadley, and were not too clear.

"I guess we've bit off a bit much," said Jack.

"Want to hear a strange one? One businessman who is a regular customer claims it's gone beyond the Christians. Some Iranians and Indians, Asian Indians, were making inquiries."

"Well, I guess I had better get back."

"Wait a second. I want to know what's going on."

When Jack was finished with his story Joe went to his closet and fished out a shoe box. "Kick the white devil's ass as hard as you can. Take this. It should get you to Rome if that's what you have to do. I'll have Thad drive you home."

When he had a chance to count the bundle of hundred dollar bills, Jack found the count was 50.

The next day there were twenty-two people crowded in the living room. A couple were there with Rain. Several young people from UC Berkeley, dropouts or on their way to being so, were there, mostly ex-catholics, and a few punks and anarchists that Cinder had gotten interested. One teenager from the neighborhood also was present.

Various people recounted their experiences in Providence, Hadley, and Berkeley. Everyone agreed that, vampires or not, it was time to hit the reactionaries as hard as possible. They would form three groups. One would go to Europe to spread the news and, if possible, locate Christ the vampire and kill him. One would set out across the United States to build the campaign nationally, only whenever possible they would stay in towns long enough to set up active anti-vampire groups. The third group would stay in Berkeley to create printed material and possibly a public access cable TV show. They would also serve as a link for any groups set up. They would operate underground, using a P.O. Box and a drop system to protect themselves. They would also move out of the house they were in and establish safe houses.

Nine people volunteered to go overseas. They decided they could afford to send four. There was a long discussion as to who would go, which ended with a secret ballot. Rain was chosen because she had contacts in the underground there and was acknowledged to be generally competent. Bayou got to go because he was dying to put a stake through Christ's heart. Oni, one of the Berkeley students, was chosen because she was fluent in Italian, French, and Spanish. The Professor and Jack tied in votes and the Professor deferred to Jack.

When they were done they had a party. They did not get drunk, and two people stood security at all times.

Chapter 9

JERUSALEM

Before leaving America their main problem had been deciding where to go. The two candidate cities were Jerusalem and Rome. Dylan's belief that Rome was the home of Christ was pretty convincing, but they reasoned that the quoted authorities may have simply been pointing at something they disliked, the Catholic Church. The Berkeley madman's opinion was given weight by the kidnapping of the Professor and Penny, plus the sure knowledge that Jerusalem had been where Christ had died. In the end they had decided to split up their forces, investigate, and call each other before attempting any action.

Rain went to Italy because she knew people there. Oni went because she knew Italian. Also, being asian, she would be subject to constant harassment in Israel. Jack and Bayou went to Jerusalem by default. They were nervous on the flight: telling themselves it was really no more dangerous than taking a drive in the U.S. did not make the possibility of a PLO attack any less scary. Neither did the idea that they were going to try to find what might be a real vampire.

After landing at Ben Gurion airport they took a bus to Jerusalem. They decided that their first job would be wandering about the city, learning its major landmarks; that would also give them a chance to see if they were being followed. Then they could check into a hotel and find a guide and interpreter, preferably someone who spoke both arabic and hebrew. Their first stop was to change a bit of money and buy a street map of the city.

"Who are those funny people with the beards and black suits?" asked Bayou.

"Hassids, at least that's what they call them in New York City," said Jack. "They live in their own world.

They're orthodox, which is the Jewish equivalent of fundamentalist. It looks like that guy is pretty pissed."

"It looks like they are listening to him, too."

A crowd of about fifty men had already gathered. Almost all of them wore glasses and nearly identical black suits. Other people, dressed in a modern fashion, were avoiding the crowd. Jack and Bayou went as close as they could get without joining the crowd.

"I wish I knew what he's saying" said Bayou.

"We'll ask."

"Excuse me, sir, can you tell me what he is saying?" After asking this to five different men a young man paid attention to Jack.

"Don't you speak Hebrew?"

"We're not Jewish. We're tourists."

"Oh. I see. He is condemning those who break the law, the religious laws. The secular Jews, women who dress improperly, people who do not keep the Sabbath. Perhaps you would like to learn more about our tradition of righteousness."

"Actually, we are looking for a vampire. Goes by the name of Jesus Christ. He never died and we believe he might still be living in Jerusalem."

"Are you crazy?" The man turned away from them.

They had been surrounded by the crowd, and now made their way out. Several men said things to them as they moved out, a couple of them obviously meant to be insulting. By the time they were safely on the other side of the street the police had arrived and were obviously ordering the crowd to disperse. The crowd started chanting and then throwing things at the police. More police arrived. Jack and Bayou retreated to the safe side of the police, a rare experience for Jack. A window was broken.

"Let's get out of here," said Jack. "Reactionaries rioting make me nervous."

Soon they were at the beginning of the Via Dolorosa, the path that Christians pretended had been walked by Christ carrying the cross that was meant to end his life.

They had read a history of Jerusalem and a Baedeker's, so they knew the city had been destroyed and rebuilt many times and that the various monuments to Christ were of modern construction, tourist traps based on guesswork and available real estate rather than Jesus's Jerusalem.

Still, they had to start somewhere, and as a psychological tour of Christianity it had its merits. They began with the first station of the cross at the El Omariye School, in the courtyard. Despite the obvious dangers of visiting Israel there were other tourists there, taking pictures of the place where they believed Christ had been condemned to death. "I wonder what he was like before he turned into a vampire," said Jack.

"Probably a nice guy," said Bayou.

There was little to see so they walked out into the street and paused by the Monastery of the Flagellation. "It must have been quite traumatic, thinking you were the rightful king of Judea or the son of god or a prophet or whatever and then be flagellated on the way to your execution," said Jack.

"I think he was scourged before he was condemned. But it sure was traumatic. People are still flagellating themselves today. I surprised Reverend Fowler hasn't revived the practice. It made quite an impression during the middle ages."

"Probably be healthier than watching TV."

The streets were quite narrow and the dusty walls of the buildings, made with native materials, gave the impression of antiquity, though most were built in modern times. They recognized the Ecce Homo arch because they had read of it in a guidebook. "I guess they had to put it somewhere, what with the original place torn down and the sight unknown," said Bayou.

Where Jesus was supposed to have fallen for the first time the street came to an end and they turned left. At the fourth station of the cross, where Jesus was supposed to have met his mother, they turned right again. Here there were more people, mostly dark skinned people who could have been either Arabs or Jews, dressed in light western garb, but they also passed a muslim women in a black gown with a full veil.

"Think of all the people who died under Roman law and have died unjustly since then. And people, children who are defenseless, taught to feel sorry for this man's execution. And to believe he is God and all the crap that goes with it."

"If the others had risen from the dead we might remember them too. C.S. Lewis said that miracle distinguished Christianity from all other religions."

"But it was a common trick at the time. At least half a dozen ancient religions we know of featured a hero who rose from the dead. The two best known are the cults of Hercules and of Osiris."

Turning left back onto the Via Dolorosa, Jack noted that there were two people walking behind them, both men. Probably just tourists, but he would keep an eye on them. Their trek continued past places where pilgrims wept their hearts out for a vampire: where Simon the Cyrene picked up the cross, where Veronica handed Jesus her handkerchief, where the Son of God fell in a most material and unmetaphysical manner, and finally to the Church of the Holy Sepulcher, where he is said to have been crucified, died and buried. They waited in the Church courtyard, and the two men waited there, too.

"You know," said Bayou, "I spent a lot of time reading the Bible when I was with the Eternal Way, but I did not think about it much. Now look at the different versions of Jesus's death and resurrection in the four gospels. In Matthew the main thing is that the high priests are supposed to spread a rumor among the Jews that Jesus's disciples went to his tomb and stole him out and said he had risen from the dead. Now that type of rumor could be pretty well squashed by a few appearances of Jesus, and of course all the Jews would have followed him. Then in Mark he just says that Jesus rose from the dead, talked to the disciples once, and then ascended into heaven. Meaning people would have to take the word of the lucky or hallucinating disciples. In Luke he appears to them a couple of times and then leads them out to Bethany and disappears, so that's the same as Mark. Then in John it gets pretty elaborate, Jesus performs some of his stock miracles and some disciples think John is promised life until the second coming, and it doesn't even say when or if he left them. It seems to me then that they knew it was a fraud from the beginning, or that they hallucinated seeing him, or saw an imposter, especially since several of the accounts say that they did not recognize him immediately. So Christ would not be a vampire, he's as dead as anyone."

"Right," said Jack, "and I'm pretty cynical about this vampire business. Still, maybe they kept Christ hidden to protect him, or maybe some vampire took over the church at a later point in time. In either case, the vampire may be here in Jerusalem. And it's true that even if we kill the vampire the church is a powerful institution and won't die overnight. We still have to try. Might as well go in the church. Tourist Trap of the Holy Sepulcher."

As they entered a group of four screaming men in black suites of the Greek Orthodox style ran screaming in one door and then out another. "Reminds me of Yellow Submarine" said Jack. Following a tourist map they headed left towards the reputed tomb of Christ. Strange noises were coming from all around them, bells, organs, and screams, but they saw no one. In the rotunda a man dressed in black, but hatless and beardless, screamed several sentences at them in a foreign language and then ran to the right. They entered the tomb through the chapel of the angel.

"I wonder if this is really it," said Bayou.

"Could be. Looks pretty solid. I doubt there's anything under it. Now isn't the time to try to find out."

When they exited a great roar was coming from the Catholicon, which was directly in front of them. As they approached it two Franciscans ran by and through its gate. Inside several dozen men fought each other with their fists. Several Greek Orthodox men formed a line in front of the altar, but soon the fray engulfed them. Jack read from the guidebook: "'The Church is actually a jumble of small interconnected structures which are the jealously held territory of disputing religions: Eastern Orthodox, Catholic, Armenian, Copt, Abyssinian, and Syrian Churches.' They must be having some kind of dispute."

"Maybe they are trying to decide whether to support the orthodox Jews or the seculars."

"Well, if we are careful this should be a good time to look around without being watched."

They exited and took a tour. While the church had many nooks and crannies there was no evidence of vampires. Then again, they did not know what evidence of vampires would be. The hill of the crucifixion, Golgotha, was completely enclosed by the church, and they looked through it. It seemed ordinary enough.

They left the church and decided to try the Scotland Inn since it sounded like a secular hotel. On the way there they saw a roadblock. They tried to find a street that was not blocked but could not, so finally they walked up to the soldiers to try to get through. The soldier asked where they were going and why, and when they answered, waved them through. The streets were almost deserted.

The hotel clerk said there had simply been a riot started by the ultra-orthodox which had led to clashes with seculars. It was becoming a common thing and there was no reason to be concerned. "Insane if you ask me," said another tourist. "Can you imagine it being against the law to drive on Sunday? Bad enough the bars aren't open."

They asked the clerk if he knew of a tri-lingual guide who might be available. Within the hour a knock at their door introduced Jeremiah Kazin.

"You can speak English, Hebrew and Palestinian?"

"My French is fair also."

"You're Jewish?"

"Yes. My father came here from America and my mother had come here from Poland long before. They are orthodox, so I am a great disappointment."

"How did you come to know Palestinian?"

"Since we lived in Old Jerusalem I learned it as a child."

"You know the city well?"

"I know the entire city."

"Are you an atheist? Be honest."

"Yes."

"Well, we're going to have to tell you what we are looking for, otherwise you won't be too much help to us. We're Americans, and one of our friends had a friend who fundamentalist Christians tried to convert . . ."

After a lengthy explanation Jeremiah said he would do what he could to help, though he had not heard of vampires in Jerusalem and was skeptical. His fee would remain the same, which was high for the budget minded Americans, but they considered it a necessary expense.

"I suggest getting started tonight, if you are up to it. Tomorrow is Friday and by ultra reasoning when the sun goes down it's the Sabbath. They don't like people running around on the Sabbath, though they aren't supposed to be out looking for you either. Things here are real tense. I don't know what has come over these orthodox. Must everyone else submit to their craziness? Maybe they are led by vampires, too."

Jerusalem is not much of a party town. By ten o'clock the streets are almost deserted. Jack, Bayou, and Jeremiah had decided on an agenda. They would explore likely places where the vampire might be buried or kept: the Church of the Holy Sepulcher, a place called Zedekiah's

Cave, and the Mount of Olives. The following night they would meet with some of Jeremiah's friends, and then they would start questioning some of the residents of the city who might know about vampires and the like.

The tourist entrance to the Church was closed, but they had not intended to enter through it anyway. They walked the church's perimeter with Jeremiah explaining how it corresponded to what was inside. They wanted to check several places, if possible. Any place not accessible to the public was a likely spot, as were any places that were low lying and potentially led to crypts.

They scaled a wall on the north side and crossed the roof, avoiding the rooftop monasteries of the Abyssinians and Copts, from which issued loud human braying. They entered Golgotha through a window with ease, posted Jeremiah as a guard, and examined the area closely for secret passages. They found none and moved together down into the Church proper. It was dimly lit, but their eyes had already adjusted to the darkness. They hugged the walls of the corridor leading along the Catholicon, which now seemed deserted, to the crypt of St. Helena. This was a comparatively large room, empty and unguarded. They searched it quickly and exited as they had come. They noted a man guarding the Pillar of the Insults. He looked at them, wondering if he should give the alarm. They walked on by while he was thinking. He guarded the pillar against the Catholic monks, not thieves.

Jeremiah led them into another corridor. "If there is anything in here that is of interest, this will be it. I first noted it when I was a child."

They went up one step through a door and then squeezed into a small room to the right. Jeremiah pointed out a grate in a wall near the floor. "If it's unguarded it can't be that important," said Jack. He pointed his flashlight into it and Bayou could see no reflection back.

"I wonder if it comes out," said Bayou as he pulled on it. It creaked. He pulled again and it creaked and opened slightly. He and Jack pulled until it opened enough for someone to belly crawl under. Bayou went first.

It was a room, undecorated, no different than the others they had been in, except that it was dirty. It seemed quite large.

"What do you make of it?" said Bayou.

"Property is valuable here. I doubt it was just over-looked," said Jack.

"People don't go in and out regularly," observed Jeremiah, "but they must on occasion or we would never have been able to move that grate."

"Well, at least it isn't filled with bones."

They looked around. The walls seemed ordinary. The floors were stone with a thick layer of dirt. "We should have thought to look for footprints," said Jack after they had left theirs all over. Then Jeremiah said something.

He was kneeling and scraping away dirt. He had uncovered a handhold. They found a second and lifted out a large tile with surprising ease. A hole led into a tunnel barely big enough to crawl into.

"Well, we've come this far," said Bayou. "Look, give me the thirty two and don't follow me into the tunnel. If I want to get out, I may want to get out quick. Wait here down in the entrance. Keep your flashlight on."

As soon as he got inside Bayou could see that the tunnel curved to the left and down. He began crawling with a flashlight in one hand and the gun in another, but quickly gave that up, holstering the weapon. There was no background noise, so his every movement seemed to thunder. Squirming a few body lengths along the tunnel, he discovered that passage opened into a room.

There was not so much dust there: the pictures on the walls were clear enough. A large marble altar occupied the center of the room. There did not seem to be any danger, so he whispered for Jack and Jeremiah to come down.

The left wall depicted, artlessly but accurately, a man being crucified. It showed a crowd of onlookers and some Roman soldiers, with a city crudely sketched in the background. The far wall showed the man who had been crucified lying on a table, with men attending to him and a smaller man or boy seated above them with a line connecting his arm to the prone man's. There was also a table with surgical instruments and, very clearly, a pot of boiling liquid beside it. The wall to the right showed two scenes. One was of the man tearing the arm off a roman soldier. The other showed men bowing before the man, who sat on a throne in the posture of a Buddha.

When Jack entered he looked around and started laughing. Bayou could not help but laugh too, but it was a fearful laugh. The man who had been crucified had a remarkable resemblance to Ronald Reagan.

"What do you make of it," said Bayou when they finally were in control of themselves.

"It's simple enough," said Jack. "They could not destroy it because it was sacred to them, but they had to hide it. If they had guarded it people would want to know what was inside. Instead they just ignored it, except to come down for occasional ceremonies. It's probably their original church. That's what Jesus really looked like, a semitic version of Ronald Reagan. He was crucified and maybe even died and then a skilled surgeon brought him back to life. Look, those are Old Egyptian symbols, not Greek or Aramaic. Not that I can read any of them, but I've seen examples. That might even be a catheter for a blood transfusion. They didn't have pumps then, so they put the boy above Christ so gravity would do the work. Then we see the results: a superman who could tear apart a Roman legionnaire with his bare hands. And them worshipping him. He really was the son of God as far as they were concerned. But he probably was no vampire, you can't keep people from aging with blood transfusions."

"Maybe you can," said Bayou. "The Red Cross sure does ask people to volunteer a lot of blood, all out of proportion to how much it's needed. Maybe some people are getting transfusions to keep them young."

"I know a lot of medical people," said Jack. "Someone would know if blood were being diverted."

"You people aren't crazy," said Jeremiah.

"Look at this altar," said Bayou.

It was composed of a great slab of the common stone of the region supported by smaller cut stones. It was inscribed with Aramaic. "We'll take pictures and get it translated later," said Jack. "No one will believe it, what with Reagan's face."

Bayou leaned on the altar and the top stone moved.

He stepped back and covered it with the gun. "What should we do?" he said.

"Normally, I prefer negotiating, but if there is anything alive in there, it shouldn't be. You used to using that thing?"

"No."

"O.K. You push, and keep your head down. Jeremiah, you keep your flashlight aimed at the opening. I'll cover it with the gun, and if it moves, I'm shooting. O.K.?"

The slab rolled easily. Jeremiah's flashlight shone into the opening. Jack stood ready.

There was nothing inside. The slab moved along grooves and stone rollers.

"He could be just out for the night," said Bayou.

"No one has been in or our for a while," said Jeremiah. "That trap door had not been disturbed."

"We should take pictures and get out. Some day we can come back with an archeological team."

They took the pictures, slid the slab back into place, and made their way out of the tunnel. They had no problem escaping from the Church.

"I take back what I said about it being a tourist trap," said Jack.

"Do you want to go to the cave?" asked Jeremiah.

"Not tonight. Do you know anyone who can develop this film for us, someone discrete and with their own darkroom."

"Sure, no problem."

"Then come by our hotel tomorrow morning around ten. We'll get the film developed, then we'll tour the cave and the cemetery. Saturday night we'll hit them again, by ourselves."

The pictures had already been sent to three separate places along with a map and explanation. The newspapers reported only briefly on the disorder at the Church of the Holy Sepulcher; the riots by the ultra-right and the demands of their leaders were the main news. Friday, the day before the Sabbath, was expected to be peaceful, so the trio set out for Zedekiah's cave. They had borrowed two additional pistols from friends of Jeremiah: if the Vampire had visited the Church of the Holy Sepulcher, they might find it. It might even be looking for them.

It was a hot dusty day. The entrance to Zedekiah's cave was just inside the wall of the Old City, near the bus station. They encountered no disturbances on the way there. They waited with a few other tourists to catch the last excursion through its depths. It was said to have been the quarry for the stones that King Solomon used to build his palace and temple. King Zedekiah and others had once used it to escape from the Babylonians. On occasion since that time it had been used for secret meetings by the Zealots, thieves, secret societies, and until it became a tourist attraction, Masons. It might well have housed vampires at some point in time, but unless there were secret entrances and hideholes that were not visible on their tour, there was no place for them to hide now.

Jeremiah knew of no alternative entrances. If they wanted to get in they would have to break in through a door opening to a narrow street. It could be done, but they did not think it was worth the effort. They made there way to the Mount of Olives, which is the ancient burial ground, and spent a few hours looking at gravestones and Mausoleums. Nothing unusual happened. They were mainly there to get their bearings.

They did not go out again until late Saturday evening. In the meantime they had called Rain and Oni, who were staying at a friend's house in Rome. Rain said they had aroused much interest in Christ the Vampire within the political counterculture, but had not actually gone looking yet. She volunteered to come to Jerusalem when she heard about the crypt with the murals, but they decided that was not necessary yet. Jack encouraged her to keep meeting with the Italians: the more people she met, the more likely they could get help in their search.

The only people in the streets were police and army patrols. The Ultra-orthodox demands included that there be a curfew on business and driving from sunset on Friday until dawn on Sunday, and Saturday several cars had been stoned in the new city. However, the Ultras could hardly enforce their curfew and keep it at the same time.

They walked from the outskirts of the Old Town down through the Kidron Valley and then up the Mount of Olives. They had no particular plan of attack: there were dozens of churches and chapels on the mount as well as a grave for almost every body that had died in Jerusalem since the Bronze age. There was a moon so they did not use their flashlights, which might have shown their presence.

"I've been thinking," announced Bayou.

"A healthy habit," said Jack.

"Seriously. What do we know about these vampires? Not much. Maybe they run the Jewish and Arabic and Buddhist religions as well. If they do, and they wanted to protect Christ, why not do it at the Dome of the Rock? Why would Christ want to be in Jerusalem anyway? Because he was crucified here? Jerusalem has been a backwater for most of the last two thousand years. Not a very good place to run a Church from, not a very safe place either. Suppose these vampires have a sort of spiritual existence and can bounce around from one mind to another. Then he might be anywhere, and killing which ever zombie he's in will just send him to another."

"So why bother?" said Jack.

"Well, we have to cover the options. I was saying about the Dome of the Rock. It's where Mohammed was supposed to be raised into the heavens. Maybe he just claimed that because he had read the Bible and wanted to capitalize on it. But maybe there is some sort of energy in Jerusalem that these vampires can use. Then maybe they would hide in the Dome of the Rock. We should at least check it out."

"It sounds reasonable to me," said Jack. "What do you think, Jeremiah?"

"I've been there often enough. I never noted any unusual energy, or vampires. It's very large, almost as large as the rest of the Old City. The archeologists would love to dig underneath it. Could be anything there."

As the hours passed they crossed from graveyard to graveyard. In most the tombstones were slabs of rough rock laying flat on the ground. There were many mausoleums, but they did not try to enter any. They avoided the Shrines and Churches as well as the crypts where entrepreneurs and religious sects pretended biblical figures were buried. They said little. To Bayou it was as if he were in a movie, an actor pretending to be in a foreign country or ancient era. Jack moved as if he were on patrol, trying to anticipate an ambush.

A body appeared walking towards them. They spread out slightly and unholstered their guns. It stopped about ten feet in front of them, a black mass a head shorter than Jeremiah.

"Good evening, gentlemen. Looking for souvenirs?" It was a male's voice in clear, sing-songed English.

"We were just looking. They say the Messiah will enter Jerusalem from here," said Jeremiah.

"That's too bad. I heard there were three men out looking for Jesus the Christ's place of burial."

"They say that's in the Church of the Holy Sepulcher. But no body was found. A lie for the Pious, most likely."

"A lie for the Pious. But the enlightened would want to find the body, not the cross."

"Are you so bold as to claim to show the body?"

"Better still," said the voice "I could show you the spirit of Jesus. At least what it has become. But suppose you relegated Christianity to where it came from, to a minor sect with a few adherents. Would not the Moslems or Buddhists or some new sect take it's place? And who cares, if all die in a nuclear war."

"We cannot jump to the top of the mountain," said Jack. "We must walk step by step."

"Perhaps you would like eternal life yourselves, if it does not involve accepting a master."

"Not if it turns us into vampires."

"There are vampires and there are vampires. You need not believe me, but I am Narcissus, once Bishop of Jerusalem. Perhaps I am demented, but I believe the body I inhabit is eighteen centuries old. Once, it is true, I feasted on the blood of Jewish children, but when I found that had nothing to do with longevity I became a vegetarian. Perhaps you would like to know the secret of life?"

"Perhaps, but we would definitely like to know if you are here to help us in our task."

"I will do one or the other. Eternal life, or aid in killing what could be eternal. But not both."

"Fair enough. Tell us why you would aid us against Christ."

"Because of the Plan. The Plan of the Old Ones. Not all old ones, but probably most of them. They plan to live forever. It won't work, but they will kill all the mortals trying. You see, they believe it is possible to live apart from the body, not simply by moving from one brain to another as some parasitic consciousnesses do. But to do this they must kill many people all at once. Disease will not work, even the most deadly diseases kill too slowly. Nothing ever worked well until the invention of bombs, especially atomic bombs. So they encourage the population to increase, and when the time comes they will start a war. They will be immortalized, and enough mortals will live to become their servants and begin reproducing again."

"And Jesus Christ is the leader in this?" asked Bayou.

"No, but Christ is important because he controls so much. He must accede to the desires of the younger old ones or they will destroy him."

"But can he be killed?"

"You can't, but you can neutralize him. He has to work through humans. Some are immortals that are kept in crypts; they are his main basis in material reality. Some are immortals who can still walk around and carry out orders. If you can kill them you can destroy Christ when he tries to enter the last one. You see, I use the word spiritualize, but it is simply the same material field that supports consciousness, only tied up in a knot so that it can exist without a body. But it can still be destroyed, I am sure of that. I'm not sure how."

"Will you help us, then?"

"I am old, and live only to see what happens. I have told you much. Now I will tell you a few more things. Killing the vampire won't stop the war. You have to get the nuclear weapons out of the hands of the governments. I don't know where all the bodies of Christ live, but if you capture one you might be able to threaten it. The ones in crypts won't be of any use, they have lost their egos. But the ones with egos will chose their own lives if that is the clear option. I'm not sure, but probably if you put them in a Faraday box Christ won't be able to control them. They will tell you where the others are. There are three that I know of, but there are more, possibly many more. None are in Jerusalem. One is Paul. He is buried beneath the Lateran Cathedral, in a large crypt. One is Cardinal Vlad. You'll never see him in pictures with the Popes, but he is always there. He's your best bet for finding where the others are. The third is in Spain, in Seville, in a castle that the Inquisition operated from. Also, I heard that Christ's original body was shipped to the United States, but that may just be a rumor."

"Can they enter our minds directly?" said Bayou.

"Only if you invite them. That is why spreading the faith is so important. People invite them, not knowing what the guest's real intentions are."

"Are they difficult to kill?" said Jack.

"Harder than a man, perhaps, but nothing miraculous is required. Just cut off the head and then cut the body into small sections. The cells are very tough, but they need food and oxygen the same as you. They have better regenerative capacities, but if the heart and head are severed the rest of the body will die too."

"What do you plan to do?" asked Jeremiah.

"Just to watch. That is all I do. And now I must depart."

The man seemed to fly or jump off to the right. They ran in that direction, but could find nothing.

Walking back they wondered whether they could believe him. "Well, if he is lying and Christ is in Jerusalem, we can always come back. At least we have something solid to go on. We might as well go to Rome."

Chapter 10

ROME

Jesus Christ the trustworthy witness,
the First Born of the Dead, and the sovereign
of the kings of the earth. -John 1:5

Rome is an ancient city and a modern one too, but most of all it is a seat of government and therefore of power. It has more in common with Washington, D.C., and Tokyo than it does with the industrial cities of Milan and Turin. It is a city of tourists, bureaucrats, students, artists, socialites and priests. It is as all other human habitations: it is heaven, hell, purgatory and limbo in the flesh.

The tour guides do not mention the extraordinary people of Rome, the ones who love, who do good work, hold the extraordinary jobs the rich think ordinary: the cleaners, cooks, children raisers, teachers, servants, typists, deliverers, thieves, clerks, nurses, construction workers, maintainers, plumbers, electricians, carpenters. It is best to love one's work when your inheritance, passed down from your parents, is to work or starve.

The anarchist tradition is still strong in Italy. It is most easily found in the great industrial cities and in the impoverished countryside, but it can also be found in archist Rome. It is not so much a matter of formal organization or even people calling themselves anarchists, as attitudes: knowing that authority is based on might, not right; that people could run things better without a government, lawyers, or rich people; that communism and capitalism are interchangeable; and that the only security is in friendship and mutual aid.

Oni and Rain were staying in a squat on the outskirts of the University District. The building had been allowed to decay by the landlord to the point where it was not possible to rent it, and it had then been seized by the city for back taxes. The anarchists had seized it for themselves, establishing the ancient rights of squatters, and defending them against policemen and bureaucrats. They paid no rent and received no service except for water. Kerosene and propane provided their light; insulation and their bodies warmed them in winter. They had put considerable effort into making the building habitable: cleaning, patching the roof, retimbering the floors and stairs. Visitors were generally welcome. Four people who denied their German Federal Republic citizenship, one person who denied German Democratic Republic citizenship, two people who denied Netherlands citizenship, five people who had by chance been born in Rome and eight people who had chanced to be born elsewhere in Italy were living there when the Americans arrived.

Rain's friend Alicia was the only person there who could be fairly considered to a political organizer. She went to meetings with other anarchists, planned activities, and handed out fliers in the streets. Her father and mother both worked in restaurants and had seen to it that she went to college. Now she too worked in a restaurant bussing dishes, part time. She did not need much money since she paid no rent. Alicia was not very interested in the Christ the Vampire campaign, it was not overtly political enough for her. But she had introduced Rain and Oni to many people.

Rain and Oni met Jack and Bayou at the airport. They did not talk about Christ the Vampire on the bus to their neighborhood. The squat appeared to Bayou as a pre-modern building with a stone facade, four stories high. The front was covered with a mural showing women baking bread in a kitchen and then the same women throwing rocks at policemen in the street. The door was not locked. As the building was filled up the men would share the room the women were in, and there they met.

"It's going quite well here," said Oni. "Yesterday I had dinner with some music students from the university who have a band. They really hate the Catholic Church and are going to write a song about Christ the Vampire. They didn't believe me about vampires, they just believe it's funny. They are cynics."

"Anyone seem to offer advice about there really being vampires in Rome?" asked Jack.

"Funny, now that I'm not in Berkeley I've reverted to my old opinions," said Rain. "I don't think there really are vampires. Maybe there will be if medical science improves, and maybe there are freaks who are unusually strong or live a bit longer than the rest of us, but vampires, no. Despite those pictures of the crypt in Jerusalem. That just proves someone knew about blood transfusions. Maybe it was a set-up, too. Because if we are running around chasing after vampires we will spend less time getting people to see what religion and capitalism do to them."

"The next time we run into one we'll try to hold it for you to examine," said Bayou.

"And this 2000 year plan stuff is right out of the Illuminati trilogy," she added. "Someone is really pulling your leg there. But since there aren't any Christians in Jerusalem it's just as well you are here. Maybe we can get some mortars and shell the Vatican."

"There go your elitist tendencies again," said Jack, laughing. "We should get a few hundred thousand people to tear the Vatican to pieces. Now that would be something."

In the end they decided to spend a couple of days seeing how many people they could actually recruit to invade the Lateran Cathedral, just in case there really was a vampire sleeping under it. After that, unless there was some other lead, they would tour Europe, spreading the word until their money ran out.

They went to eat dinner in the communal kitchen. There were no rules regarding buying, cooking, eating, paying for, or cleaning up after food there except the one written on the banner spread across the fireplace, which translated into "carry your weight."

"Isn't this wonderful?" said Oni. Being from the American middle class, suburban variety, she had never seen an old fashioned kitchen with huge cast iron implements, a tank like stove, and a massive wooden table that could seat twenty. "We cooked last night with Gunter. Sometimes no one cooks, or people just cook a bit for themselves, but its fun so usually a bunch of people help made a whole lot of food. Rain says there are places a lot like this in Berkeley. I want to live in one when I get back."

Jack felt so good he wanted to hug all humanity. To somehow let them know they could be free and loved and wise and without illusions. It was a warmth he could not communicate except by smiles and deeds. He set to helping.

The next day those in the household who were not out working were aroused by a woman yelling, in Italian, "Quick, at the Coliseum, people are going crazy. They say it's the Anti-christ!"

The woman was gone before Oni could talk to her, but two other people from the house said she had said something about a man flying and preaching against Christ and government. The six of them decided to go to see what was causing the commotion. They set out immediately for the Via Cavour. Everything seemed normal enough in the street: traffic flowed as usual, there was no evidence of hysteria.

They saw the helicopters before anything else. There were at least three, one a police chopper and the others from the media. Before they came into view of the Coliseum they began seeing police officers directing automobiles away from it. Then they could hear the choppers and there were other people moving towards the ancient building, the top of which was soon visible to them. They asked a young man what was going on as he hurried towards it. "They say the Anti-christ is giving out gold coins," he said, and broke into a run.

A large crowd had gathered and with it several hovering helicopters. They edged into the outskirts of the crowd and only then had a figure pointed out to them, floating in the air near the Coliseum above the crowd, wearing a white robe. It was a man, for he wore a beard, and his skin and hair were dark. Rumors swept the crowd and Oni did her best to translate them. The man was either Simon Magus or the Anti-christ, and had floated in the air giving a lecture against Christ and the Church. Then he had started giving out gold coins until the affair had become disorderly, and since then he had floated in the air, appearing to meditate.

Jack could see no obvious method of trickery. The man was very far out from the building and much too high and immobile to be supported by wires.

"I am Simon Magus!" The words were loud, they could hear even over the roar of the helicopter.

"I have dwelt among mankind for 2000 years this day. My body and soul are incorruptible because they are the Truth and the Godhead. I am here to teach and to warn. Heed my words.

"The world is wrapped in Darkness and Madness. No man or woman is safe from the hatred and superstition of the powers of darkness that rule this world. You believe in false religions. Your priests do not heal the sick, they tax the living. Your politicians seek glory and wealth, not your good. The strong among you prey on the weak, and the strong nations prey on the weak nations."

"You believe Jesus is the Son of God. You believe he is the Prince of Peace, but you are always at war. I tell you, I was there, I saw it, he did heal the sick in his lifetime. But he is dead! His followers wish you to believe he is alive, but he is dead! I dare him to appear! He is not in heaven, he is not on earth. Charlatans rule the gullible in his name. They say he is in heaven, and that he talks to them, and you must obey."

"You can live forever, I am the proof of that. I followed the true path, the path of truth and to truth, and was united with the First Force, the Eternal Light, the Creation Spirit. My body that walks among you today is two thousand years old. It is not destroyed with cancer, it is not decayed by microbes, it is alive. And now I warn you.

"Follow the path of Truth, seek true union with the Godhood, study with my disciples who are now among you, and your will survive the coming cataclysms. Stay with the Pope and the Bishops and Priests who prey upon you and if you are lucky you will die as your ancestors died. But the Pope and his friends ready an Apocalypse for humanity, and it can be escaped only when these powers are overturned.

"Another windy preacher, you think. But can you float in the air? Can you fly? Can you heal the sick by the touch of your hands, can you turn copper into gold? I have demonstrated these things, and they will be demonstrated again in good time. Now tell the world what you have heard and let all look at themselves and judge themselves."

The figure grew increasingly brighter until they had to shield their eyes from it, and then the light dimmed quickly and Simon the Magician was not to be seen.

"That's funny," said Jack. "Why did he make his speech in English."

"Maybe for the global audience," said Bayou.

"But it was not in English," said their friend from the house. "He spoke in Italian."

All six of them cursed at once.

"Hello, are you Rain?" said a stranger who approached them. She was short, almost as short as Oni, and had long, straight black hair and olive skin. She looked perhaps twenty years old.

"It's O.K.," she said, "My name is Helen. I'm a friend. Wasn't Simon Great? He flew once before in public in Rome, and later the Christians spread a rumor he had fallen to his death. They were always best at propaganda, the Christians. We'd like to help you in your work. We know an entrance to the catacombs beneath the Lateran Cathedral. I'll meet you tonight at eleven where Via Merulana meats Via Labicana. Is that O.K.?"

"Sure," said Rain. "Is your friend Simon . . ."

But the woman had turned and disappeared into a crowd.

"Funny how miracles always appear in the distance or the dark," commented Jack. "She disappeared into the crowd the same way I would if someone were following me. Too bad she didn't use that blinding light trick."

"I suggest we meet her and pretend to go with her tonight so that we can learn where that entrance is," said Rain. "Then we can go back in our own good time. It might be a trap."

They agreed that nothing more could be done there.

As they walked back their friends questioned Oni at great length about Christ the Vampire and whether Simon's appearance meant that Christ was really dead and Simon was the Vampire.

"It's a cloudy day," said Jack. No one returned his comment.

"It you really wanted too," he continued, "you could suspend yourself from a helicopter. A feedback system controlling the helicopter, fixed on the ground and the person being suspended, could keep him floating there without moving. The light could be magnesium: you would not notice the man being pulled away, or maybe the man was a dummy filled with magnesium."

"Jack, the going is getting weird and you're not turning pro," said Rain. "We heard him in English and they heard him in Italian. It can't be done with technology. It had to be some form of mass hypnosis."

"I wonder what the TV cameras recorded."

"There's a TV at the house."

The TV cameras showed the man floating there, close up, but they had recorded no speech at all. The man had not moved his lips, though the camera crews heard the speech. Interviews conducted on the ground missed the fact that people heard the speech in different languages, and everyone attributed differing versions of the speech that were reported to the frailty of the human memory.

They prepared as best they could for their meeting. Rain and Bayou would go to the meeting, armed, along with two anarchist volunteers. Jack would work with Alicia to coordinate their cover, which included several people from the house and others Rain and Oni had met. Oni would stay by the telephone booth near the house; someone had to get out alive if things went wrong.

They did not wait long before Helen appeared. "Good, you are armed. But is this all of you? It is a dangerous thing you are doing."

"How dangerous?" said Rain.

"I don't know. We have not been down there. We believe one of Christ's bodies is down there. It acts as the center, directing the others. We don't know how many there are. They may be zombies, the undead, but they might also be living humans. You must presume they are armed, and there may be traps. They may also be able to bend minds, to confuse you. They all can be killed with bullets, and I advise you to shoot first and ask questions later."

"And are you a vampire, Helen?" said Rain.

"I am incorruptible, which is not the same as being undead. I do not prey on other people. I am a teacher, like Simon. We know the vampires, we know what they are doing. We are only in a position to help. Seek the truth, and be brave. Let's go."

They walked. Rain asked how Simon had done his magic tricks, but Helen would only say that he knew the elements, and therefor could command the elements.

When they were in sight of the Lateran Cathedral she pointed out a metal cap that covered a culvert. "This is the entrance; the sewer is dry except after a rain. Inside about twenty meters towards the Cathedral, on the left is a large grate. If you push on it hard it should open into a crawlway to a ladder that goes down to the first level of catacombs. After that I don't know the exact route, but you must head towards the Cathedral. You can get lost, but if you wander about you can find other exits to the surface. They may be barred, but you could use your weapons. There could be traps, but I doubt it. The real danger is the guards."

"Are you coming with us?"

"No. I have other roles to play. May you find the truth." Helen walked off, leaving the others standing there.

Jack and his friends started tracking Helen. She walked openly down the street. Two trailed her and the others ran ahead in anticipation of her movement. When an empty taxi came along the street she hailed it, and they lost her.

By the next evening they had a total of eleven people willing to go vampire hunting. The episode with Simon Magus had made everyone take the situation seriously; they knew there was danger. They had flashlights, knives, pistols, compasses, tools, and three semi-automatic rifles. They decided there was no way of keeping a line of communication back to the surface, so they would all go in. They agreed they would have to shoot anything that seemed to threaten them, since they did not know the powers of their enemy. Two teams of three would alternate as point and follow up. A team of two would carry the main responsibility for orienting, and another team of two would cover the rear.

After midnight the first time there was no traffic they pulled off the sewer cover. Three of them went down, found the grating, and opened it. One went back to call for the second team of three to follow. When the first team confirmed that there was a ladder leading downward the third team followed. They carefully paced the distance, checked the compass, and marked their position and depth on a map. They also painted a glow in the dark arrow back towards the exit. Only then did they call the rear guard.

Since Rain knew how to use the submachine gun and had a cool head she was in the first group with a German autonomen and a Sicilian anarchist. Oni was one of the mappers, along with an architecture student. Jack was in the second group with two anarcho-communist women, and Bayou was in the rearguard with Alicia. The Sicilian, Mario, was the first to drop down into the catacomb. Rain climbed down the ladder with one of the automatics when he said it was clear. Only when she could cover him did he examine the room. There was a stone staircase going deeper: as soon as they got word that the others were ready they went down it with the same caution.

Their progress was slow, but they did not relent in their caution. As best they could they made their way in the direction of the Cathedral. Mostly the tunnels they moved through were not catacombs, or at least did not have obvious tombs attached to them. Sometimes they would enter a relatively large room and twice they found sarcophagi and waited while the second team opened them to find skeletons. When they became tired they traded with the first team. It was four A.M. when the mappers sent forward word that they were nearing the Cathedral. They were forty meters underground.

It was cool but Rain was soaked with sweat from toting the machine gun and its ammunition. She had tied a bandanna around her forehead to keep the sweat out of her eyes. The constant contrast between the darkness and the flashlights was also straining her eyes. She guarded a passage that led to the right from the main route. When the mappers caught up she would rotate forward.

She heard a noise and realized it was music. Straining to hear, she decided it was coming from her corridor. Oni approached. "Go ahead and tell the others to come back here. Tell them to keep quiet."

They could not hear the singing when they had gathered, but they decided to try the corridor. The first team went back to point. The second team would be close behind them. The mappers would guard the exit where they had come from until they had to move forward. The rearguard covered what had been the forward corridor.

Rain went first, after an argument with Mario. She turned off her flashlight, which was strapped to her forearm. She could see a bit ahead from Mario's flashlight; he was close behind her. She kept her footing steady and her gun ready to fire. The tunnel curved slightly to the left. She could not see the end.

Meter after careful meter she took the ground. Then she sensed there was light ahead. Carefully she signalled Mario to turn off his light. When he did it was clear that they were moving towards a flickering light. She could hear no singing.

There was a room ahead. It was empty, lit by an oil lamp in the wall. Each of its four walls had an opening to a passage. With Mario covering the room she eased along the wall to the left. The singing chant was now coming from its opening, but she could see nothing down its hall. The other two halls were quiet and dark. She returned to the one on the left and signalled for Gerhard, the autonomen, to enter and cover the one across from Mario. Then the women entered and covered the final door and the room from one of the corners. Mario joined Rain at the point and then they had to wait for Jack to run back to bring the others forward before relieving Gerhard.

Again Rain moved down a tunnel. Soon she could make out that light came from the opening at the end. The singing became louder and she could smell some sort of incense. She moved forward until first the opening to the room and then the far wall of the room came into view. She leaned to the right and left, could see little more. She moved forward another step. The singing came from a larger room beyond the first. Again she leaned in each direction. This time she thought she saw someone standing in the room to her right. She inched forward for a better look. It was a man in a black cassock armed with a submachine gun. She signalled to Mario.

She entered the room firing: the man flew to pieces. Mario was already flying into the room beyond. There was a brief instant of silence, without the chanting, before Rain heard Mario's gun burst. She ran into the room behind him. Several white robed figures were rushing Mario, and she fired at them. Other white robed shapes were fleeing out a door. They were in some sort of chapel with a simple stone altar. Gerhard leapt over the corpses and covered the door.

"They are zombies," said Mario, looking at one.

Rain too looked at its face. It had no eyes and its skin was eaten back to the bone of its face.

"Shoot them through the head and the heart. We have to move quickly. Bring the others forward and keep covered."

He ran for the door and Rain followed. Caution was as dangerous as incaution now: time could only work against them. The corridors were dimly lit and branched frequently, meaning they could be surrounded and cut off. After about three such intersections they came to a large room that was clearly a dormitory from the beds. Shots rang out when Mario jumped into the room. Rain knelt and fired at the far door.

"Mario?"

"They missed me. I think they retreated."

"Cover me."

Rain dove into the room and under a bed. Again there was silence. She wormed her way under the beds until she had a fair view of the far hall. Then she rolled to the center. The hall was empty. She charged forward.

Another intersection, but clearly the main hall led forward. She did not cover the intersection. Another large room, this one painted with scenes of torture. Another hall. More gunfire, only now it was behind her. She lay down. Mario went back. Time passed, marked only by occasional gunfire from pistols. Then bursts of automatic gunfire. Then Mario was back. He did not tell her that the architecture student was wounded.

There was fire towards her from up ahead. She could do nothing but return it. Again Mario left. She interchanged gunshots with the darkness, trying to conserve her ammunition.

Then there was heavy shooting ahead of her and then silence. Mario yelled at her from ahead now. She called back to him, got a response, moved forward.

It was another chapel. Two red uniformed guards, humans, not zombies, were dead on the floor. A child was naked and dead on the altar. Doors went to each side, and an opening several shoulders wide led forward.

It too was a chapel, a sepulcher. The slab of the sarcophagus had been taken off. A pool of mucous like substance lay at the bottom.

On the walls was a depiction of the sacrifice of a circumcised baby boy. There were also pictures of Christ on the cross and seated on a throne.

"They moved him."

"Look, there is a trail of the slime."

Again they set off, more cautious now. The trail led back to the chapel, then to the right, down a staircase, and then back in the direction from which they came. They followed it down a rough cut tunnel.

Suddenly a chasm opened in front of Rain. Far beneath her ran a stream. Perhaps twenty feet across the chasm the tunnel continued. The bridge that had led across had been destroyed.

"We'll have to turn back."

Mario took a look and then agreed with her.

They had a hasty conference back in the sacrificial chapel. They could look for another way to get to the trail, but by then either the vampire would have retreated beyond their reach or fresh troops would be sent against them. They began the long march back, guided by their fluorescent arrows. It was harder on them than the advance, for they were worried about an ambush and were tired. People were already walking the streets when they pushed the cover off the manhole and emerged. They were beyond caring.

They slept the next day. The Americans called home and then talked to their European friends. They agreed that Oni would stay in Europe and the others would join the Christ the Vampire campaign, both spreading the word and organizing another attempt on the thing that had lain beneath the Basilica. Rain, Jack and Bayou prepared to return to their native land.

Chapter 11

THE SKULL

John Jefferson was figuring about what Gordon said. If they were serious about forming their secret society, then they should use a real human skull. It wasn't a question of magic: John did not believe in magic or religion either. The skull was to refute magic and superstition.

John knew and liked each of the kids in the group. Most were lifelong friends, and all of them belonged to the high school Science Club. They were, John thought, the small group of young people in Shiloh, Virginia who lived in the 20th Century, not the Old Testament. Most society initiates had parents who did not belong to the Southern Baptist majority in town.

Gordon Wilson had thought up the secret society and the skull. Gordon was the school brain and a major thorn in the side of the school and religious authorities. In addition to his being a Wilson his mother was a Carter, so ninety percent of the white people in the county were related to him one way or another (as were most of the black people, though the Carters and Wilson's would never admit to that). He looked like most of the Carter/Wilson/McCarthy clan that occupied the area: blond hair that was slowly turning darker as he aged, bleached blue eyes, a square forehead, and a small chin. His father was the lineman for the electric utility, so it wasn't too surprising that he was so good at math and physics. His mother worked for the Post Office.

"We have to have some sort of opening to the average person," Gordon had said, "something anyone can come to and learn from. Maybe someone who doesn't buy the whole biblical dog and pony show, but who still wonders if Jesus performed miracles, you know the type. Someone who really needs to know about evolution and the real history of religion. But we also have to purposefully undermine the Christians, and that has to be a secret, done with people we trust. You know if they have half a chance they'll do an Inquisition on us. You know what they did to David Carter."

So, they formed The Friends of Darwin. To further the society's ends was not clear, but the important thing, Gordon told John, first was to bond them together. All secret societies had ritual initiations. A human skull - that would do it. Dead people weren't in heaven: they were dead. So taking someone's skull did not hurt anyone. It would be both illegal and sacrilegious, cementing their secrecy and solidarity.

All nine of them attended the first trip to the graveyard. Matthew, Randy, Lauren, Steve, Gordon, John, Jimmy, Carol, and Cathy. It had taken a lot of discussion to get to the point of action. It was up to John, of course, to start to shovelling.

The blade of the shovel broke through the grass into the soft black soil. John put his foot on the back edge of the blade and thrust it all the way in before swivelling the handle down to break the earth's hold, and then lifting the shovel and soil to toss the dirt off to the side. His arms trembled slightly, but he plunged the shovel back into the earth. By the time he had moved five scoops of dirt Randy had joined him. Soon they were warm despite the cool air, and broke into sweat. It quickly became hard work. They had not dug down twelve inches when John asked if anyone else wanted a turn.

Carol took the shovel and after that everyone wanted a turn. They were digging up the grave of Jonathan Edwards, whose worn gravestone sat in the oldest section of the church graveyard. According to local legend he preached the town's first Baptist sermon and according to his tombstone he had been born in 1799 and died in 1892.

"Hey, I hit something hard," cried Lauren. Cathy was digging too. They stood in a hole over three feet deep. They both stopped.

"Well, it's not likely to be the coffin, it would have rotted by now. Let's keep digging."

"Sure, but I'm tired. Someone else want a turn?"

"Yeah," said Cathy, "someone else can take my place."

In five seconds it became clear that no one relished volunteering.

"O.K., I'm rested up," said John, and he leaped into the pit, which was only a bit over four feet wide. "You want to help me, Gordon?"

"I wouldn't miss this for the world."

To John's surprise he almost immediately hit a hard object, and soon Gordon did too. They made a little hole, brushed back the dirt, and got a flashlight handed down.

The light illuminated flat, polished, white marble, somewhat stained by the soil.

"It's marble. Christ, they put him in a marble coffin. Must have been an important guy."

"Great, the skeleton should be perfect."

"We were just going to get the skull."

"Sure, the club can have the skull and I'll take the rest of it. Wow, this is great."

Gordon's enthusiasm dampened with his shirt as they realized that their hole did not match the outlines of the crypt. They had excavated too far from the headstone and at least a foot to the left. Fortunately some of the others got used to the closeness of their quest and then got bored and volunteered to take turns.

It was close to 2 A.M. as they positioned themselves to try to raise the lid. John and Gordon waited at its head while Randy and Matt pried open their end with a tire iron. Once they got their fingers under the lid and positioned the four of them heaved at once and the lid went right up on internal hinges.

Flashlights shown down into the coffin from above and one of the boys screamed as Matt simultaneously scrambled out of the pit.

Gordon and John just stared. A man lay in the coffin, looking fresh as BHA preserved sliced bread. He was dressed in a plain, black, old fashioned suit with a white shirt. His lean and weathered face had plenty of gray hair and a long beard.

They half expected him to move. He just lay there.

"He must have had one hell of a mortician."

"Something's wrong," said John at last.

"No kidding, John," said Cathy from up above.

"The smell." That was Gordon.

Right. It didn't smell like decay or like formaldehyde either. It smelled like someone who needed a bath.

"Get out of the pit," said John, turning to Gordon and Randy. "And get the rope from my car."

John could not help but look at old Jonathan while waiting for the rope. The preacher really looked as if he were sleeping. He lay on some sort of cloth or pad. He wore black, old fashioned shoes. All of his clothes looked 19th century.

When they brought the rope John tied it around his waste. Then, very carefully, he squatted down beside the casket.

"Someone's coming," Jimmy squeaked.

John thought he heard the footsteps of someone approaching, but when he focussed on his hearing he heard nothing. Instead he felt someone approaching. He fought down panic.

"A couple of you better stop whoever it is before he gets here."

Everyone else was talking at once. John decided to let them sort it out and to look at the miracle of preservation before he lost his chance. Up close the man looked alive, sleeping, though there was no movement and the skin seemed waxy. John touched the black clothing. Someone was coming very close, and a few of

John's friends had run away and the others were saying "come on, John, let's get out of here." John reached and touched the man's face.

The man's eyelid flicked open.

John stood up and half jumped, half was pulled by the rope out of the grave. A few feet away Jimmy was writhing on the ground, whimpering "No, No." John felt a great pressure in his mind, as if a foreign presence were trying to invade it.

He turned to the grave, and the man had closed his eyes. He was just lying there, motionless. John swept a flashlight around the area, but could spot no intruder. Suddenly Jimmy jumped up and ran off.

"Help me close that goddamn casket," he said, finally.

"Are you crazy?" asked Cathy.

"If we don't close that casket, we're all going to be."

There were only three of them now, John, Gordon, and Cathy. Cathy and John got back in the hole and lowered the lid of the coffin. Almost immediately they all felt better, and they scrambled out. John and Cathy went to work with the shovels and Gordon scooped dirt back into the cave with his hands and by kicking it. Lauren came back and helped, reporting the others had left. They refilled the grave in half the time it had taken to dig it up; they left long before dawn.

They met three days later in the abandoned Humphrey's shack. Of those who had been at the grave, only Steve was missing.

"O.K.," John said, "something very surprising happened the other night. But the real world can be weird. There's quite a few explanations. But let's start with observations. Different people saw and felt different things. Why don't we just go around the room and Gordon is going to take notes so we can refer to them later. Who wants to start?"

No one volunteered. "O.K.," John resumed, "I'll start. Things were pretty much as we expected at first, but we found a marble coffin, which I think was real unusual in those days, the 1800's. We opened the coffin and there was a very well preserved man inside. We were all scared and I stayed in the pit and got a rope tied around me in case the man turned out to be alive or something. Then Jimmy said someone was coming and I thought I heard someone coming, but when I concentrated instead of hearing I more felt someone was coming. Everyone was panicking and I decided to have a look at the man and I touched him. Then I felt a big pressure on my brain. Then I touched his cheek and then I thought I saw him open his eye. His left eye. Then I jumped out of the pit and everyone was gone except Jimmy was crawling on the ground and Gordon and Cathy were there. The man's eyes were closed and so we put the lid down and spent a couple of hours refilling the hole."

"What about since then?" said Jimmy.

"Well," said John, "I guess sometimes I've felt as if I were being watched. And I woke up from a bad dream last night, but I couldn't remember what had happened in it."

"O.K." said Gordon, "no one want's to go, so let's go in a circle. Cathy is next."

"Well, I saw the man, I was holding a flashlight. But I didn't hear anything when Jimmy said someone was coming. People running off made me scared, and I wanted John to get out of the pit. Then John jumped up. Then I was real scared but I helped put the lid on. I think the corpse was well preserved and we just got spooked."

Randy went next. "Before Jimmy said anything I thought I saw something and was trying to look over towards the church, but I didn't see anything. Then I saw a big dark shadow coming, and someone else started running and I ran too. To my car and I came home. Yesterday I was day dreaming and I thought I saw some- one floating in the air, but that woke me up and there wasn't anything."

"I saw the corpse and it sure was well preserved," Lauren said. "It didn't smell like there were any preservatives. John told me to get out and I did. Then Jimmy and the others thought something was coming, and I did too, but I just figured it was a person and we would have to do some fast talking. Well, I wanted to run, but John was in the pit. Then there was the panic and everyone ran except Jimmy was kind of having a fit on the ground. John was real close to the corpse and then he was trying to get out and I hauled on the rope. Then I ran to the cars, but I went back. We got the grave filled back in." He paused. "Last night I had a dream. I was sitting in a field and people walked by carrying crucifixes and they were all happy, but there was something wrong with them and when one came over to me I got scared and woke up."

The other teenagers told consistent stories, except for Jimmy.

"I guess it must have been like going crazy," said Jimmy, "or maybe taking drugs and hallucinating. I heard something and then I saw a man who looked like Jesus walking towards us. I was scared but he was saying reassuring things, and he came right up to me and touched me and then it was like a bad dream, I was struggling to wake up. I was out by the highway, I don't know how I got there, must have walked or run. No one else was there, so I walked home. Now I keep having dreams, I'm afraid to sleep. Jesus keeps coming and telling me I can live forever if I accept him. I'm scared, but when I'm in the dream I'm very tempted, because I don't want to die."

"Jesus is dead," said John. "It's just a bad dream because we all got scared. I was the only one who saw the man, and maybe it was Reverend Edwards, saw him open his eye. Maybe I imagined that. But we all saw the marble coffin and the corpse - hey, maybe it wasn't a corpse at all. Maybe it was a wax impression!"

"Yeah, like those wax museums!"

"Sure, the guy had a duplicate of himself made. So he got a marble coffin to protect his investment."

"And anything could have made the noises - an animal or the wind or even someone hanging around the church."

Pretty soon everyone had worked out an acceptable version of what had happened and they cheered up, even Jimmy. They decided to declare the Friends of Darwin official and swore an oath of secrecy. They made the grave digging their first official adventure and again swore they would tell no one about it. They decided not to make further plans yet, but to meet again in a week. They voted forget the skull business and start studying the area's ecology.

The next day John, Cathy, and Gordon had a chat after school.

"Jimmy had a bad dream last night again. His sister told me." Cathy said. She was the star biology student that year, a McCarthy and daughter one of the town's few Presbyterian couples.

John, his ivory teeth contrasting to his dark face, spoke slowly, as if he wanted to hear his own voice and keep it in control. "Something is going on. People are agitated, on edge. There were two fights yesterday. There haven't been two fights on the same day in a long time. And the ministers are revving up the flocks, at least at the black churches."

"All the more reason to start fighting back," said Gordon. "I got this magazine, Fact Sheet Five, and it lists all the little magazines, they call them zines, that are put out in America. I wrote away for samples of some. All we have to do to make an underground paper is write some stuff, put it together on sheets of paper, and get it copied at the Copy Shot. If it's four pages they'll cost twenty cents each. Two hundred will cost about $40. We could give one to everyone at the school."

John liked the idea. "O.K., the Friends of Darwin can do that. You propose it at the next meeting. That's only a few dollars apiece. At the meeting we can decide what should be in the paper and who's going to write the stuff."

"Great. I'll bring the zines I got to show the others. Most of them are about music, but what they show you is that it can be done."

"We've still got two big problems," said Cathy. "We have to help Jimmy. I guess just spend time with him. His parents go to First Baptist and he has to go to services and Sunday school, so he's having a lot harder time than us."

"We hang out with Jimmy anyway, I guess we'll just have to spend more time with him."

"The other thing is Reverend Edwards' body," said Cathy. "We'd better have a look at it. I checked at the historical society, there's no record of there being a wax body made. It's still the most likely explanation, but if that was a live man in there, we'd better find out. It's always important to know the truth."

John shied away from the idea. "It can't be alive. And it's a lot of work, digging up the grave again. I don't think the others will be much help."

"She's right, though," said Gordon. "It has to be done. If we have one other person, we can work in shifts of two. At least this time we can go straight down to it, and the dirt'll be soft."

"I think Randy will help. He feels bad about running last time."

"What if he is alive?" John fumed. "What are we going to do then? Jesus, he must be some sort of vampire."

"Or he's in suspended animation," said Cathy. "We'd better have a couple of guns with us, just in case, and a can of chloroform to knock him out if he's able to do more than just blink his eyes."

"What if someone finds us?"

"Don't you even watch TV? This time we'll put up trip wires with bells, and have lanterns in addition to the flashlights."

Silence.

"We have to," said Gordon.

"Alright. I can get my dad's .32 automatic pistol," said John.

"Knowing the truth is worth it," said Cathy.

When they went to find Jimmy he had already gone home. At his door he said he had to study. They did not press him because his mother looked over his shoulder, giving them the evil eye. The moment the door closed they could hear her loud, shrill voice being thrown at Jimmy.

Friday night came and they set out to dig out the coffin. Randy came with them and brought a second gun; Cathy stole the chloroform from the biology lab. They set up their trip wires and bells, then began to dig. It was easier this time, the ground was still soft from the previous dig. "Think of it as archeology," Cathy said.

They hit the marble coffin almost exactly this time. Cathy and Gordon prepared to raise the lid while Randy aimed his gun where he figured the Reverend's heart would be. John sulked but did his duty, standing guard against the night, dying with curiosity but not looking at the coffin.

They lifted the heavy lid.

The coffin was empty.

"What the hell," said Cathy.

"Someone must have taken it. Someone must care about it," said Gordon.

"There's not much we can do. Say, let's get samples, you know, of the coffin and the lining inside. Maybe we can learn something from that."

"Sure, then let's get the hell out of here."

The stars were fading quickly by the time they were ready to leave. They had all come in Randy's car. As they opened the trunk a man stepped out of the twilight towards the car.

Sheriff McCarthy smiled into the flashlight beam.

"Find anything?" he said, grinning.

"No sir," said Gordon, feeling sick.

"Jimmy Snopes told his parents you all were out digging up the cemetery. You know people around here might get right mad if they thought you were disturbing their relations. I told them I would take care of it. I did you a favor."

"Yes sir."

"Now if I catch you poking around here again I'm going to take you to jail and have your parents come get you. I don't want to do that, but I will if I have to. If you want a skeleton for your science club I recommend you order through a catalog. Then you won't be disturbing folks around here."

"Yes, Sheriff McCarthy."

"What about the rest of you."

"Yes, Sir," they said in unison.

"O.K., you can go, but remember you owe me a favor."

Jimmy was the only person missing from their next meeting of the Friends of Darwin.

"You should not have gone without us."

"How many of you would have gone?"

They all raised your hands.

"How many of you would really have gone?"

Matthew and Lauren lowered their hands. "I think I would have," said Carol.

"It's alright, next time you should ask. Nobody has to do anything, so it doesn't hurt to ask."

"You're right. We all have to stick together. Look what happened to Jimmy."

"I heard he saw Jesus. You know, born again."

"I tried to talk to him and he said 'Jesus loves you,' but he looked afraid."

"Living with his parents must have driven him over the edge, that and whatever happened to him that night. It's almost as if something got inside him. That's when we stopped feeling it."

"Cut that out," said Gordon. "Nothing was there but our fear and nothing got inside him. His parents put fear and loathing inside him starting when he was a baby. His rational side held it down for a while, but now its got a hold of him. Until he gets away from his parents he's probably a lost cause."

"I'm still having dreams," Lauren interjected. "They won't go away."

"What are they like?"

"It's like a man, I suppose it's Jesus, but I don't know. Anyway it's like I'm a child, and he's offering me things I want, like candy or toys, but I'm afraid of him. Then he always says 'You don't want to die, do you? You're afraid of dying, aren't you?' Then he grabs me and I wake up struggling."

"Well, it's just a dream, but maybe it would be good if someone slept over with you." John was trying to speak calmly. "The thing is we are a tiny minority in this town, and there is constant pressure to conform. We have to stick together and we have to wake people up. That's why we're going to start an underground newspaper. Gordon, tell them about it."

They chatted happily when the business part of the meeting ended. They spent hours working on articles for the paper together.

That night John fell asleep as usual. He was a deep sleeper and seldom remembered his dreams. In the middle of the night, though, a noise woke him up. Someone was banging on the window. He figured it had to be Gordon or Randy or one of his other friends. He looked over and saw that his brother was still fast asleep. The banging started again. John threw off the blanket and went to the window, opening the curtains.

It was Reverend Jonathan Edwards.

John stepped back from the window, his heart in his throat. If it was a dream, he thought, he'd better wake up.

The man motioned him to open the window. John looked at him closely, seeing that the man seemed fully alive.

"I want to tell you something, John," the man said, and John could hear the voice through the window.

John considered. If the man really wanted in, all he had to do was break the window, or any of the other windows in the house.

John decided maybe he could open the window a crack, and armed himself with his baseball bat.

"That's right, open the window," the reverend said. "You want to know the truth. The truth is you can live forever. Come outside with me and I'll show you."

John snapped himself out of the trance. Instead of cracking the window he closed the curtains and thought of getting his dad's gun, and instead reached over to wake up his brother. But the man's shadow disappeared from the curtain; John carefully peaked out. The reverend was gone.

John did not sleep the rest of the night.

"There's only two explanations. Either someone dressed up as the Reverend to give us a scare, or the Reverend is a vampire. Or whatever you want to call something that rises from the dead and lives underground." Lauren was certain.

"You know what the sermon was at the churches yesterday? Eternal life for those who believe in Jesus, hell fire for the damned. And the apocalypse is coming on earth, more or less. Every church in town," Carol said, "every single one."

"If someone who looks like the Reverend is around, how come we never see him?" Randy was not convinced.

"He sleeps in a coffin in one of the churches," explained Matthew, the chief proponent of the vampire theory. "His friends dug him up."

"I think everyone is getting a bit jumpy" said Cathy. "Look, it was a mask or makeup. Someone knows about the Reverend, whoever it was who dug up the wax body. Either they noticed that the site had been disturbed, which wasn't too hard to see in the day time, I'll bet, or they learned from Jimmy's parents. They are trying to scare us. They're scared of rationality, scared of science, scared of us thinking for ourselves, and they work through fear. Fire and brimstone for the gullible, social ostracism for the skeptics."

"Maybe we should tell our parents," suggested Randy.

"Sure, we'd get a lot of sympathy there. Our parents don't want trouble."

"Is it like this everywhere?"

"I don't think so," ventured Gordon. "Most American's don't go to church on Sunday. I'll bet in the big cities there are lots of atheists and people who just don't care."

"Well, at least we have all the stuff for the paper. Monkey's Skull, what a great name."

"I've been thinking," said John. "Let's not get it printed at the copy shop here. They are bound to look at it and remember who brought it in. My dad said I can go to Hadley with him this Saturday, so I can get it copies there. Then we can put them in everyone's lockers, slipping them in through the vents, so no one will know who did it."

"Like they aren't going to guess it's us," said Cathy.

"They won't know for sure."

"Is anyone opposed to the idea?"

"Alright, that's the way we'll do it."

Saturday, walking around the few blocks of downtown Hadley, John noticed a sign spray painted in an alley. "Jesus Lives" it said. Underneath it a rectangle of grey yellow paint obscured something else, and gazing at it he made out the outline that had also been spray painted, in another hand: Vampires Never Die.

He began to wonder if the whole world was mad. He had been planning to go to State, if they recruited him for his baseball skills. He began thinking things might be better at some school up north. At least he had not seen the vampire Edwards since that first night. But he must be out there somewhere.

Gordon seemed obtuse when they talked later.

"Look, he rose from the dead," said John. "He caused Lazarus to rise from the dead. He wasn't the son of god. He was a vampire."

"I guess my idea about getting a skull for the Friends of Darwin wasn't so hot," said Gordon. "Everyone has gone bonkers on me. Look, probably Jesus existed, but he never brought Lazarus back to life and he didn't rise from the dead. They just added those stories later on to impress the gullible."

"Why don't you sleep over at my house tonight? We'll both be safer."

"Sure. Look, I'm going to hand out Monkey's Skull tomorrow. That should take the pressure off the rest of you. My home situation is different. My parents aren't always totally reasonable, but they don't feed me any religious bull."

"I wasn't dreaming about the Reverend. It was a real person."

"I know it was, John. And if a real person breaks into my house, if I don't kill him my father will."

"I'll pass out the zine with you."

"No, I want to do it myself. I'll take them home with me when I go and give them out first thing in the morning."

Fortunately the first thing that happened when the teachers realized an unauthorized zine had been distributed was that they tried to confiscate them all. That assured that most of the students carefully hid their zines and read them as soon as they could. The principal called Gordon into his office and threatened to expel him. Gordon threatened to sue, and left the office victorious.

That night Gordon woke up. Someone was pounding on the window.

He got up, went to the window, and pulled back the curtain.

It was the Reverend.

Gordon started to raise his hand to the switch, and the room went pitch black.

He hurt. It was like no pain he had felt before, because it came from everywhere, one massive swelling of hurt that almost drowned out his existence.

He opened his eyes.

Images swam into focus. There were men in front of him, old men dressed in robes, as from the middle ages. They looked at him with keen interest. Two of the men were old, wrinkled, almost deformed. The third he recognized as Reverend Edwards. Further away were two soldiers dressed in leather and metal. Light came from two torches set in the wall.

"Francus de Franco, renounce the Unitarian heresy. Accept the Father, the Son, and the Holy Spirit. Save your soul from hell and your body from death. Renounce."

"There is only one God." This came from a mouth that was Gordon's and not Gordon's. Gordon realized he was hanging by his arms, his feet suspended from the ground. Everything else was pain.

"Behead him," said the old man who spoken.

Gordon screamed.

His hand was almost to the switch, and the Reverend smiled through the window, his eyes locked into Gordon's, penetrating into Gordon's mind.

Gordon's hand flicked the switch.

A hypodermic needle slammed into the man's body and a 60 cycle current grabbed the man's nervous system. Gordon went outside carrying his father's gun in case the Reverend had friends, but no one else was in the yard, so he turned off the electricity. He tied the Reverend up, gagged him, and blindfolded him before bothering to find out if the Reverend was dead or alive.

After a few seconds Gordon heard a single slow heartbeat.

He dragged the body into his room, the only place his parents would not discover it in the morning. Then he called the number he had found in one of the zines.

"Hello?"

"Is this the Committee for Public Safety?"

"Yes. Who are you?"

"Gordon Wilson. I'm calling from Shiloh. I caught one of them. A vampire."

"Look, uh, Gordon, I don't want to disappoint you, but we've investigated six people who've called us about catching vampires and three were pulling our legs, two had captured ordinary human beings and one was a set up by some Christians who almost killed one of our people. Hold on . . . someone else thinks they have a vampire."

A different, faint voice said "where are they calling from?"

"Where did you say you were calling from?"

"Shiloh. Virginia."

"Where's that?"

"About 50 miles outside of Hadley, which is ..."

"He's near Hadley."

A different voice asked Gordon what had happened. Gordon told his story.

"Are you sure your vampire is secure?"

"I have him tied with ropes and sedated with sodium pentothal."

"You and your friends put him somewhere secure. We have some people in DC. They'll probably come by to help you in about four hours. We've never caught one before. We don't know what their powers are."

Gordon had a good idea of the reverend's power, but in his mind he began to devise a series of experiments.

Chapter 12

THE PENTAGON

Lieutenant Reyems was a good salesman. He was just over six feet tall and well proportioned, big enough to impress most people but not so big as to scare them. His hair was too short to let people know it was more red than brown, and his eyes were too blue to be scary. Mostly people saw only the uniform and his face with its delicate chin and heavy brows.

His life had been shaped by many things, but mainly by a satellite named Sputnik. Launched by the Soviet Union in the year of his birth, it had caused intense panic in ruling American military, industrial, and political circles. They realized they had gone too far in purposely lobotomizing the American public: to compete with the Russians they would need more and better scientists, engineers, and technicians. They would have to spend more money on schools, even for the lower classes, and emphasize science and math more. They would have to convince parents to push children in this subject. It would be dangerous, of course: if children learned to think for themselves as part of the scientific process, they might also think for themselves about politics and economics. It was a necessary risk.

It also meant a space program, a heroic effort that required a goal, which eventually became to put men on the moon. All over the country in the early 1960's children decided they would grow up to be astronauts. John Glenn was the national hero. As time passed most of them changed their goals, realizing that astronauts were few and standards were high. But not Tom Reyems. True, he wavered at times. He could have done better in high school. He learned the horror of the Vietnam War, he was ecstatic that his lottery number saved him from being drafted, he indulged in alcohol and drugs, he nearly flunked out of college. Then he realized that he would have to do something with his life. He worked harder and got better grades his last year in college. And he decided there was a way he could still be an astronaut. He could start by flying jets for the army.

He checked into programs and found basically the same deal in all the services: with a college degree he could sign up and become an instant officer, with a seven year commitment. He really did not want to be in the army, it was looked down upon by virtually everyone after the defeat [let's face it, America was big, bad, a bully, and still got its ass kicked] in Vietnam. But getting into a top graduate school in a science, the only other route he knew to his goal, was out of his reach. He had no desire to go into business, which was also looked down upon by his generation. He signed up with the army. He told his friends he would refuse to fight if a war came, he was just doing it to learn to fly jets, to become a test pilot and then an astronaut.

A year later he was flying helicopters. They had not told him that those who did best in flight school would get to fly jets, and those who did second best would fly helicopters. Later they sent him out for a gig as a recruiter. He did well, he liked it fine, and after another round flying helicopters he did it again. Ten years later he was an old pro.

He had worked in a variety of places: small towns, big cities, the South, the West. It was always the same: slow, except for the first couple of weeks after high school graduation. The size of the place did not matter. In the cities they mainly got the poor black kids with no where else to go: the poverty draft. In the countryside, the small towns, they got everyone who wanted to split town and was afraid to do it on their own.

Lieutenant Reyems was a good salesman. He gave people what they wanted. If they wanted reassurance he reassured them. If they wanted excitement he promised excitement. If they wanted travel he guaranteed them travel. To the job seekers he gave jobs, to the skills seekers he gave skills. He was there to help. It was an easy job. He even refused promotion he liked it so much.

All over America they came to the recruiting centers. Few were inspired by patriotism, though all were patriots. All were Americans looking for the best deal they could get. Perhaps they had failed in school or were lacking in spirit. More often they wanted to escape the place they had grown up, whether it was a ghetto or a strict, domineering family. They took some tests, asked some questions, signed, reported for service when and where they were supposed to, were clipped and examined.

A few cc's of blood. Some went to the base lab and was tested for type and signs of disease. One cubic centimeter was frozen and forwarded with the others to the Blood Sample Section in Arlington, Va. But this was only a transhipment point to a place nearby: the Pentagon. At intervals a white van would make the delivery. A sergeant would always be there to take it in a dolly. He would walk to an unmarked elevator that few people knew the purpose of and fewer still had a key to. The elevator sped downward almost putting the sergeant in free fall for a moment. It crushed him to the floor as it stopped.

The two armed guards in private uniforms eyed him without the hint of recognition in their faces that normal humans would have. Yet they recognized him and let him pass without a word. He walked down the hall, pushing the blood laden dolly. He passed by doors until he came to one that looked like the others. He removed a key from his pocket and unlocked the door. Two more of the guards were inside. Beyond them was a massive steel door which was not locked. The massive bolt slid easily at his touch. He stepped inside a steel lined room, still pushing the dolly. There was yet another door to the room, but instead he pushed the dolly over to a small wall safe like door. He unpacked the blood, opened the door, and placed the blood in the chamber. Then he took the dolly and packing out of the room, past the guards and back to the corridor. The trash he placed in a container for that purpose, the dolly was placed in a utility room. Then he went back to his room, which contained a cot and a desk. He opened his bible and began to read where he had left off. The words were in Greek.

The blood's deposit was duly noted by its assignee. He activated a switch that would sterilize it with gamma rays. Then he opened the chamber from his side, removed the blood, and put it in a large freezer. He took part of an older batch out of the freezer before closing it.

He put several cc's of the blood in a special breast pocket to warm it to body temperature. Normally he would have done nothing until it was warm, but now he lay down in his recliner. It was specially designed so that he could make himself vertical enough to encourage his body to stay awake, but still have his weight comfortably supported. He focussed his mind on Reverend Jefferson of the Holy Zion Batbit Church in Anacostia.

When he had the Reverend's attention he projected his thought: "Does anything trouble you, Isaic?"

"Lord! All is well but one thing. This servant does not wish to trouble you with it. It troubles me, this evil in my neighborhood."

"Tell me, Isaic. Let me salve your troubles."

"Lord, someone put up signs in the neighborhood. They said it is a vampire infested area, and that Christians are vampires. We took the signs down, but people are disturbed at this hideous blasphemy."

"Do you know who put up the signs?"

"No Lord. They must have been put up late at night, when our good flock would be sound asleep."

"Listen, Isaic, this is the work of Satan, but it is carried out by his followers on earth. You must double your vigilance, for the Second Coming is near, within your very lifetime. These people may be back, to spread their lies, or they may be putting up the posters in different neighborhoods. Organize your people to look for them. Capture them and turn them over to Reverend Bob. Do you understand?"

"Yes master, it will be done as you command."

Withdrawing from the communication trance Jesus reached for a syringe. He took the warm blood from his breast pocket and, one by one, stuck the ampules with the needle and filled the syringe. When that was done he uncovered his leg with its special device for keeping a vein permanently open. His practiced hand slid the needle into the device and made the blood his own. Malcolm "Wireman" Johnson saw the two men putting up the posters. It was late at night and the posters were small so they were probably leftists. All the people who advocated armed revolution put up their posters in Wireman's neighborhood because there had been some pretty major rebellions there in the past. Sometimes the old folk talked about them, they called them riots, but mostly he had learned about them from the leftists, who called them rebellions. He listened to everyone, that was Wireman's thing: he had listened to leftists, preachers, pimps, policemen, social workers, shop owners, bums; anyone who wanted to talk. He had done some reading, too, and learned from that, but mainly he liked talking with people.

When they had gone on down the block he took a look at one of the posters. It read:

VAMPIRE ALERT

Warning! This area is known to be infested with vampires.

They may look human, but can be recognized by these signs:

(1) Desire to control other people's lives.

(2) Blindly follow the orders and suggestions of their vampire masters.

(3) Inability to think for themselves.

Note: it is not true that vampires are hurt by sunlight or are afraid of crosses. Also, they live off people's spirit, not blood.

This area is particularly heavily infested by followers of Christ the Vampire, a magician born in Judea approximately 2000 years ago. The Roman government attempted to execute him by crucifixion, but he rose from the dead and began preying on people. Victims of Christ the Vampire have visitations from him or his closest followers including Mary, Queen of Vampires, and follow their instructions without thinking. They are known to be dangerous and will purposefully try to make new vampires, even their own children.

> Dr. Van Helsing
> J. G. Eccarius
> Committee for Public Safety

Wireman just stood there, figuring. O.K., Christ rose from the dead, and that's what vampires do. But Christians aren't vampires. Saps, maybe, but not vampires. Preachers weren't vampires either. So it was a joke. The Christians would be hopping mad. And the people who put it up must know that. So they must really dislike Christians. Which was easy to understand. Lots of people in his neighborhood did not like Christians, and some hated them. The women especially seemed to get hot about it. No wonder there, either. Being able to get contraceptives and abortions meant not being forced to marry some jerk or go on welfare. They were nice to your face, Christians, but they would call you sinner behind your back and vote for jerks and their children really caught hell.

That was a nice touch, too, about Jesus appearing to people. That would make the born-agains think twice. He had already tried asking them, though, why they were sure it was Jesus who was appearing to them. They weren't likely to be swayed by stories about vampires. He would check up on it in a few days.

The next day he could tell from the way the Christians looked that they had either seen the posters or heard about them. Denise Cooper, who was a morning person, said that all the posters had been torn down by 8:15 when she went to get a donut and coffee. "Lines" Washington reported that he had read one of the posters around 5:30 AM on the way home, and had a nightmare as a result. "Lines" wanted to know if Wireman wanted to do something about the vampires. Wireman explained it was a joke.

The usually pasted on smile face of Mrs. Toomy had changed to a frown.

"Something wrong, Mrs. Toomy?" inquired Wireman.

"Ain't nothing wrong," she snapped back. Wireman had never heard her say "ain't" before.

Wireman at times roamed around the entire city of Washington, D.C., but he spent most of this time in his north-east quarter neighborhood. Within a few blocks of the apartment where he lived with his mother and sister were a half dozen or so churches. Only one, the Batbit church, looked like a traditional church. The others would have the ground floor of a building or sometimes just a basement floor. They were mainly Charismatic and had small followings. There was not much in terms of mainstream churchgoers in the neighborhood. Either people did not go to church, or they were pretty passionate about it. Also there were muslims, but their church was further away.

The next day he saw his friend Danny, whose parents were both active in the New Church of the Holy Temple, which emphasized strict adherence to scriptural ethics rather than charismatic rebirth. Danny was fourteen years old and torn between obeying the authority of his parents and living a life of his own. He was one of the best students in school because his parents always made sure he did his homework.

"Hey Danny, what's happening? Hot enough for you?"

"I like the heat. I don't see why everyone complains so. What are you up to?"

"Just scouting around. How's the family? Are they still making you study during vacation?"

"Two hours a day. But are they pissed the last few days."

"Yeah? What did you do?"

"Nothing to do with me, except I'm the whipping boy. Some people put up posters about Christ being a vampire and some of the children had bad dreams. I didn't see the posters."

"So what are they going to do?"

"Get ticked off at the least little thing. Also they are having a meeting at the Church tonight about it. Just the elders, us common sheep aren't invited."

"So what do you think, Danny? Is Christ a vampire? You should know."

"Vampires are Satan's agents. Everybody knows that."

"And you'd sure know if your parents were vampires."

"They're strict but they aren't vampires."

"Then again, if they were vampires, you'd be a vampire too, and you couldn't let on to me."

"Cut it out Wireman. That's not funny."

"O.K. Let's go spy on that meeting tonight."

"I can't do that Wireman. I've got to watch my brothers and sisters. My parents would kill me."

"Well how can you know for sure? I mean, they sure do teach you to follow orders, just like the poster said."

"You saw the poster? What did it say?"

"It said vampires can't think for themselves and let the ministers tell them what to do. Sounds like your parents. Sounds like you if you don't watch out."

"I'm not a Christian. I've been thinking. I have to stay with my parents until I go to college. I've got to pretend."

"Then tell them you promised to help me with my math. Your sister Darlene can watch the kids. She's done it before. When is the meeting?"

"I think it's at seven. I'll tell them I said I'd meet you at six thirty. I'll tell them it's to help you get a job. Call me at six and I'll tell you if it's cool."

The meeting itself was mainly a disappointment. It was just the same stuffy people they knew reassuring themselves that they were righteous and should continue to hold their heads high in the neighborhood. It was suggested and accepted that the posters had been the work of the devil who had probably operated through drug dealers. Parents whose children were having bad dreams would be told to tell their children that it was the devil in disguise and that Christ loved them just like their parents did. A suggestion that the children be beaten was resolved against.

Time passed and Wireman turned his attention to other things. It was a couple of Sundays later that he saw Matt Gibson sitting on a bench when he would normally be in church.

"Say Matt, where's it at?"

"Hey there, Wireman."

That was a dismissal, but Wireman was curious. "Nice morning. Nice to relax outside on a Saturday when you have to work all week."

"It's Sunday," said Matt.

"Oh, is that right? I lose track when I'm not in school. That's right, Mom was home yesterday. Guess it's Sunday. What time is it?"

"Nine forty two."

"Say Matt, aren't you late for Church?"

"I'm not going."

"Something wrong, Matt?"

"Yeah, something's wrong. I make four dollars and twenty five cents an hour and the store owner is getting rich. I should go back to school but I was never very good at school. I don't have a penny to my name, and the preacher said that was as it should be. Every week I've been making $170 gross and $123.17 take home, at least since my raise, and I've given $17 to the church. That's, what's four times seventeen?"

"Let's see, its sixty-eight."

"Sixty-eight dollars a month."

"And what's twelve times sixty-eight?"

"Shoot. It's ten times sixty eight, that's six-eighty, plus two times sixty eight, that's, uh, one thirty six, so that's something like eight hundred and ten dollars."

"Right! Eight hundred and ten dollars. I'm going to start saving the money so I can either put down a downpayment on a house so that I don't keep throwing away rent to the bloodsucking landlord, or maybe I'll set myself up with a store. It will take years, but it's better than dying poor."

"What about your soul?"

"Be damned if I'm going to stay with those blood sucking vampires! I had a dream. I know it was just a dream, but it was Jesus and he was with the Reverend and they were counting my money and laughing. Laughing!"

"Now if you could just stop paying rent and taxes, you'd be in great shape."

"You're right there."

As the summer wore on church membership began to decline. At first it was people who were going to church just to socialize or to be more highly thought of in the community. They did not like it when people started making vampire jokes: drink a good dinner, last night? Or noticed that mirrors were not allowed in Churches. Mostly, however, it was the children, because they had believed in Jesus and the crucifixion and resurrection and now they had nightmares. They were scared to go to church and some of their parents stopped taking them.

Somebody painted "Vampires" across the front of one of the churches one night. That Sunday attendance at the church dropped by one fifth.

The leftists were taken by surprise. People started listening to them and asking them questions, if not actually following them. The New African People's Organization, the Black United Front, the African People's Socialist Party, Communist Worker's Party, and Revolutionary Communist Party all thought their day had come, though they did not think to connect the surge in interest with the vampire campaign. They sold more of their newspapers, but they did not actually recruit more members.

"What do you think of these revolutionary parties? You know them, don't you?" Matt inquired of Wireman.

"I've talked with them. Funny, they're all pretty much the same, but they don't get along with one another."

"Well, the Black parties say we should separate and the white parties say we have to unite with the white workers or we can't overthrow the government."

"That what you want to do, Matt, overthrow the government?"

"I don't want to have to pay rent, and I don't want to have to pay taxes. I don't want to have to mark up food a hundred percent at the store so Mr. Boss can get rich."

"Well," said Wireman, "this is the way I figure it. These revolutionary parties all want to be the government, and maybe they'd be nice to us for a while, but they'd be running things, not us. They'd like running things and would make sure they kept running things, and then they would start rewarding themselves for it, making us pay more taxes, and soon we'd be right back to where we are now, except maybe not as poor and maybe blacks will be fully accepted."

"I'm not fighting for that," said Matt. "On the other hand, I'm not getting in their way."

"Seems to me that we should be in control. Like it's our neighborhood, the buildings were built a long time ago, so why should we pay rent? And why pay taxes or take orders from the government? What we should do, and all the other people should do, is just take control of our neighborhoods and our workplaces. Then if something needs to be done on a larger scale than a neighborhood we can appoint a commission to get it done, only when it's done the commission gets closed down. Otherwise it would get to be like a government."

"What if the Russians invaded?"

"We'd fight them. But I don't think they would. They have enough trouble keeping their own people in line. Hell, they can't even conquer Afghanistan."

"Makes sense. But how are we going to do it? Without one of them revolutionary parties that will become a new government?"

"Set up a secret society to do it."

"Is there one?"

"I don't know. But you might ask Rick Little and Little Bobby Hutton. They were asking the same thing."

Yes, things were moving and stirring in Washington, D.C., but no one, not even Wireman, knew what it meant. Mostly people just went to their jobs and then back to their families. But the Civil Service Commission got increasing reports of typists and such talking back to their superiors, and around town people were talking to each other about things besides the summer re-runs.

Weeks later school had started again and Wireman had been approached by two secret societies and asked to join. One, the Association of Free Students, which was mainly political, sought to make students aware that the school was a dictatorship and at the same time there were more exciting things to learn besides what was assigned in school. They said it was inspired by the student societies in South Africa. He joined the Association to learn what was going on. The other was the Committee for Public Safety, named after the group who had put out the Christ the Vampire fliers, which sought to save students from Christian parents. He joined that too, for the same reason.

He had begun to watch the national news on TV for the first time in his life and in late September there was a surprise. Reverend Fowler's church in Hadley was reported to have caught fire. Since it was made of stone it was burned out rather than down. The next day's newspaper reported that the children in the Christian Academy adjoining the Church had set it on fire. It did not say why. But it was easy to guess.

Two nights later he heard sirens and saw fire engines. He hurried to the fire. It was the Batbit Church, and the fire engines were already hosing down adjacent buildings while waiting for the uncontrollable fire to burn itself out. Wireman figured it was either the Committee for Public safety or a similar group had set the fire, but there was no way of being sure.

By the following evening every church Wireman walked by had people from the church standing guard in front of it. Wireman figured that, with the congregations getting so small, keeping a guard posted would wear out congregations pretty quickly. Meanwhile, churches started burning around the country. There was a riot that started in Berkeley and ended in Oakland and saw five churches burned down. It was not reported on the TV or in the Washington Post, but the left wing papers carried it.

Another day passed. Arriving at school he noted a tension. The police had arrested the main people in the Committee for Public Safety in dawn raids that morning. There were extra policemen around the school, too.

Someone suggested they had better have a meeting. Someone else said then the police would know who the secret members of the Committee were. "We are everyone, just about," Wireman informed them. "All we have to do is go from classroom to classroom and tell people what happened. We'll stop classes until they release the prisoners."

"Let's get the Association of Free Students to call a strike," said a female member of the Association.

"O.K., let's go." There were eight of them. Classes were due to start within minutes, so they gathered their friends as quickly as they could. When the halls cleared and classes started they went from classroom to classroom. First some teachers tried to stop them, then the police backed by the basketball coach and team tried, but some of the teachers and most of the students supported them and within an hour they had control of the school. They spent the day arguing about what was going on and what they should do as they watched larger and larger numbers of cops gather outside. In the end they decided to march through the community and continue the strike the next day.

The police tried to stop them but there were too many students. They argued about whether to march on the sidewalk or in the street, but there were so many of them the argument was settled by physical need. The police watched but did nothing. The students weren't sure what to do, so they chanted "Free Our Committee" and "Free South Africa" a lot, marched maybe twenty blocks, and went home.

Wireman was feeling better than he ever felt. He heard of meetings to plan the next day's activities, but did not go to them. He walked around the capital. Something was going on: there were police everywhere and soldiers had set up roadblocks around the White House. The Capitol was sealed off too. He stopped and talked to people, but no one knew what was happening. He asked a soldier, who just said "We just got orders not to let anyone by here, and not to talk to anyone."

The five o'clock news was just as useless. They reported the roadblocks, which were around other buildings and the Pentagon as well, but did not know who had ordered them. The national news only added that martial law was declared in the District of Columbia, but that everyone should report for business as usual the next day.

Then he heard the megaphone, first as just a blur, then as a voice, then as a pattern of speech, and finally as understandable words: "This is the police. Marshal law has been declared. There is now a curfew from 8PM until 6AM. Anyone in the streets during these hours will be detained. This is the police . . ." The sound reached a peak and he imagined the car in front of their building, then it trailed off as he pictured the car moving down the street. He immediately went downstairs and into the street. Quite a few people were already there, and more were coming.

"What's this about, Wireman?" It was Mr. Taylor and some other neighbors.

"Martial law. That means they suspended civil liberties, which means they can do anything they want. Arrest you without a warrant. Hold you without charging you. That kind of thing."

"So what's new about that?"

"It just makes it easier for them."

"But why?"

"Must have been that riot in Oakland. It's not a war or they would have told us. Hell, we'd be half way to boot camp by now."

"But on the TV they said it was just Washington D.C. Why us, why not Oakland?"

"Obviously they aren't telling us something."

"They just announced the President is going to address the nation at nine o'clock."

"Wonder how they intend to keep people off the street."

"They're going to arrest you, fool."

"Not if there's enough of us."

"What you going to do, stay out on the street just to prove a point?"

"Maybe, depends what the President says."

"Say, everyone," said Wireman, "we had a strike at school today because they arrested some of the students last night who were with the Committee for Public Safety. They may try to break up the strike tomorrow. Sounds to me like tomorrow is a holiday anyway, what with martial law and roadblocks and all. Maybe you could all come to the school to support the strike."

"Sounds like a good idea to me."

"Say, maybe that's what this is about."

"What, martial law because one high school had a strike and a march? They didn't even break a window."

"No, no, the vampires! My cousin in Jacksonville said they burned a couple of churches there and the Christians firebombed some places too. The president is a Christian. Maybe he's trying to save the churches."

Wireman slipped away from this group, which had swelled to fifteen people. He went and listened wherever he saw a large group. Sometimes he told people about the school strike, but other people must have had the same idea, because everyone was talking about it. A few groups of people wanted to put up barricades in the streets or start burning churches. A group of Christians guarded its church, another talked of supporting the

President. When the police patrol came again along a main street people started throwing bottles and rocks at it and it sped away. Eight o'clock passed without incident. Towards nine people started moving back inside to see what the President had to say. Wireman went back to watch the TV with his mother.

The President was sad but firm, concerned but reassuring. Domestic violence incited by anarchist and terrorist organizations against churches had gotten out of hand, and was traced to a conspiracy with liberal politicians within the congress itself. The President regretted having to arrest sixty three Representatives and nine senators, but the situation was now under control. Those arrested would be given a fair trial, and the governors of the states would appoint their replacements as usual, with elections to follow as designated by state laws.

"If they haven't been tried yet why are they being replaced," said his mother.

"Must be guilty," offered Wireman.

In addition the country would be under martial law until the end of the following day. Troops were being mobilized in case the conspirators were coordinating with foreign powers. Two divisions of infantry and one mechanized division were patrolling Washington D.C. to insure that no coup against the constitutionally appointed powers would take place. Then the President appealed to God, patriotism, and the flag.

"Honey, I don't think even white people will believe that."

"Mom, they don't have to believe. All they have to do is wait. Why do anything today, when you can do it the day after tomorrow when martial law is suspended? And ten to one they extend it for another twenty four hours tomorrow."

"You're right son. I hear there is a strike at your school tomorrow. Is it still on?"

"Yes Mam."

"Well, I'm going to skip work and come and watch. I don't want you hurt."

Wireman hugged his mother and then went back to the street to see what was happening.

When the shooting started it was mostly among the troops themselves. The crowds weren't actually attacking them or throwing rocks, and most of the troops had a good idea of what was going on. So when their commanders ordered them to fire on the crowds, most refused or purposefully aimed into the air. On the occasion that some of the men or their officers did actually shoot at people, it turned into a firefight among the troops. Probably more officers and NCO's died than civilians. The soldiers had been trained to follow orders, but there had always been the presumption that the orders were legitimate and they would be fighting foreign armies, not American civilians.

The news black outs that had been standard practice since the middle nineteen seventies had worked against the Christians. By the time the U.S. actually started a war in Central America none of the people against the conspiracy believed it, much less rallied to the patriotic newsclips shown on TV. When people got no news, or false news, they assumed the worst. When the long distance telephone system was cut off after the fifth day of martial law and people could no longer find out what was happening from friends or relatives most assumed the government was in its last throes and churches were being burned everywhere. They also believed that everyone who had ever muttered a complaint against their boss or voted Democratic was being arrested, tortured or executed. In fact only a few thousand people were executed by the government and right wing and Christian death squads, though hundreds of thousands were arrested and held in stadiums overlooked by machine guns.

So when Wireman marched with the great crowd to the Pentagon an armed soldier walked at his side.

Almost all the soldiers joined the crowds or simply went AWOL once the President, the rump Congress, and their retainers were evacuated to Camp David. As usual, Wireman got his man talking.

"Think there will be trouble at the Pentagon?" asked the soldier.

"I was going to ask you that," said Wireman.

"I hope not. I haven't had to shoot anyone yet. My friend Travor said that a squad over by some administrative building shot their Lieutenant after he shot a soldier because they all refused to fire on the crowd."

"We didn't start this thing. Maybe people should not be burning churches, but the Christians started telling everyone what to do."

"Funny, I was raised Christian, and I guess I believed it until a couple of weeks ago. Hell, I even told my friends I saw Jesus because they all said they did. Then all the sudden people started saying Christ was a Vampire, and I got all hot, and then I said, what the hell, I never really believed it anyway. But I did believe it. It's as if I'm another person. I never would have shot unarmed civilians, though. That's not why I joined the army."

"You can see it now."

"Funny, I've never seen it before. It's my first time in the city. It's pretty big, isn't it?"

"Think they'll defend it?"

"Well, they probably feel they can't defend the country if they let us in there."

"What if we tell them we won't hurt anything, we just want to see if they are really hiding the vampire in there, and to make sure they are not helping the President and the other traitors."

"Sounds reasonable to me, but then I'm not them."

"Well, good meeting you, I've got to go talk to someone."

Wireman threaded his way through the marchers, trying to get to the front. He knew who would be there:

the petty Bolshevik types. They would pretend they were leading the crowd when they were merely preceding it. Indeed, as he approached the front he could hear them chanting slogans. Old, tired slogans.

It was a sunny, cool day, a rare thing in Washington. The Pentagon stood in its white majesty skirted with tanks and soldiers. Soon the reds were yelling at the soldiers.

Wireman spotted a reasonable group of people towards the front of the crowd: they weren't joining in the red's shouting. "Let's walk on around the Pentagon," he suggested, "we have plenty of people to surround it and these reds don't know how to talk to people."

It probably would have happened anyway, so Wireman did not congratulate himself on being the leader, he just did not want to take chances at this point. Within half an hour the crowd had surrounded the troops and stabilized its line about thirty yards from the troops. A good distance: not apt to scare someone into shooting unnecessarily, but showing a serious intent.

When he was ready Wireman took off his clothes except for his briefs. He walked slowly towards a likely looking group of soldiers. "I just want to explain why we're here."

"Shoot him if he comes any closer."

"Why don't you let your officer shoot this unarmed civilian himself. Look, there are soldiers in that crowd. They realized the President was trying to become dictator and the people of this country weren't going to allow that to happen. If you shoot we'll shoot back and it will be a bloody mess. But we didn't come here to hurt you. We just heard that Christ the Vampire is protected here and we have some business with him. All we're asking is that you turn him over to us. In a few days you'll realize that you are obeying orders from the wrong people. But today we do want that vampire, if it's here. And if you don't give him to us we are coming in to get him. Just take a look at your fellow soldiers in that crowd. If you don't believe me, ask them."

"There's no vampire here," said the officer.

"You haven't looked yet," said Wireman.

"Why don't we let them look, Lieutenant? I sure as hell don't want to shoot at them."

The Lieutenant looked at him, and looked at the soldiers in the crowd, and at the crowd.

"I'll ask the Captain."

An hour later the Lieutenant reported that the commanding officer said no.

"I'll tell the people that you refuse to give up Christ the Vampire. You soldiers should come with me. Obeying that officer's orders is treason now, because it's public knowledge that the President committed treason by falsely arresting members of Congress. It's come with me or shoot those innocent people out there. Except those soldiers out there may shoot back."

"I'll court marshal anyone who abandons his post!" screamed the Lieutenant, as most of the men started to leave.

"Stop or I'll shoot."

One of the men turned around and leveled his gun at the officer. The men who remained with the officer did nothing. "It's over, Lieutenant. We aren't fighting until we know who's in charge, and it sure isn't the President. You can come with us or you can stay." Then the soldier lowered his gun and walked calmly into the crowd with the others.

Soon people were fraternizing all along the line. At a few points people even began entering the building.

An hour later people were beginning to conclude that there was no vampire in the building.

One of the clerk typists finished struggling with her conscience. "I don't have the key," she said, "but you should check that elevator. Sometimes people come in and go out from down there, and, well, they are a little bit weird."

The art of persuasion was no longer adequate once the revolutionaries got the elevator to work. The subterranean guards had stationed themselves to shoot into the elevator when it opened. Several people were wounded, two seriously, before they got the doors closed again.

Back at the surface, after taking care of the wounded, there was considerable deliberation. They got confirmation that the people in the bunker were not in the regular chain of command. It was decided to throw a hand grenade out of the elevator. Even so there was a firefight in the hall outside the elevator.

When they broke into the final chamber no gunfire waited for them. The Vampire looked at them gently and said "There is no need for violence. In fact, I have been kept here against my will. I'd be happy to come with you."

A NOTE ABOUT THE THIRD PRINTING

The first two printings of *The Last Days of Christ the Vampire* contained numerous typographical errors and deviations from standard spelling. In this printing these mistakes are corrected, at least in part. The author made some additional minor corrections. The major difference between this printing and prior printings is the inclusion of "The Skull" herein as Chapter 11. The first half of "The Skull" originally appeared in print in *The Stake #1*.

Some Alternative Information Sources:

MAGAZINES

THE STAKE, c/o III Publishing, P.O. Box 170363, San Francisco, CA 94117-0363. Humor/Horror for a dying planet: stories and essays in a satirical vein. Sample $3.95; four issue subscription $12.

ANARCHY, c/o C.A.L., P.O. Box 1446, Columbia, MO 65205-1446. Single issue $2.00, six issue subscription $8.00. Every three months Anarchy brings you alternative news, reviews, lists of contacts, and essays that explore the limits of authority and autonomy in our world. Topics include sexuality, ecology, and of course, anarchy.

FIFTH ESTATE, P.O. Box 02548, Detroit, MI 48202. Single issue, $2.00, three issue subscription, $5.00. An anti-technology, primitivist journal that consistently challenges the preconceptions people have about the nature of our civilization. Always interesting.

EARTH FIRST! POB 5176, Missoula, MT 59806. Single issues are $3.00, one year's subscription is $20. Truly radical environmental journal. For those who prefer to save the environment rather than just talking about it or praying to slimeball politicians. No Compromise in the Defense of Mother Earth!

PROCESSED WORLD, 41 Sutter St. #1829, San Francisco, CA 94104. Single issue $3.50. Consistently funny satire and social commentary, often about office workers, computer programmers, etc. Learn about how Amerika runs from people who see it as office peons working in the centers of power and greed.

There are lots of underground and alternative magazines published in the U.S.A. and the world; the problem is finding out about them. *Anarchy*, listed above, reviews a good number of them in each issue.

UNDERGROUND & SMALL PRESS BOOKS
(mail order):

Even as we go to press for the third time with The Last Days of Christ the Vampire you can't buy it in most bookstores. Because of the interlocking connections between the corporations owning the big publishing companies, the distributors, bookstores, the library system and the major publications that review books, it is practically impossible for an independently produced book to get in front of an audience in the USA. However, in addition to a few great bookstores there are mail order houses that specialize in providing obscure titles to the public. Here are some of them:

LEFT BANK DISTRIBUTION, 4142 Brooklyn N.E., Seattle, WA 98105. A complete mail order catalog of anarchist, anti-authoritarian and counter-cultural literature.

AMOK, 859 N. Virgil, Los Angeles, CA 90029. Have you ever wondered if maybe, somewhere, a few men are controlling the world? A catalog of paranoia, conspiracy theory, truth posing as fiction, and good unclean fun.

LOOMPANICS, P.O. Box 1197, Port Townsend, WA 98368. A catalog appealing to individualist and right wing anarchists, with useful information for all: weapons, tactics, finances, technology, fake i.d. and tax avoidance, and lots more.

FLATLAND, POB 2420, Fort Bragg, CA 95437-2420. An interesting selection, mostly fiction, from smaller, independent book publishers.

@DISTRIBUTION, 339 Lafayette St., Room 202, New York, New York 10012. Informative catalog of anti-establishment literature.

LAST GASP, 2180 Bryant Street, San Francisco, CA 94110. A complete catalog of underground comics, plus music books, t-shirts, etc.

HUMOR/HORROR FOR A DYING PLANET
from III Publishing

VIRGINTOOTH   by Mark Ivanhoe $7.00
Elizabeth is the newest vampire in town, a shadow who, like her
fellows, is present at every human death, waiting to feed upon
the energy and memories of the dying. She dwells in a world of
illusions, sampling the lives the other vampires have created for
themselves. But the vampires' world, like the human world, is
coming apart at the seams, in an apocalypse very different than
that expected by Christians.

THIS'LL KILL YA   by Harry Wilson $6.00
What is killing the town's censorship committee? Could it be
Satan, or their own evil hearts?
"An entertaining and thought provoking book."
                - Writers' Workshop
"Apocalyptic Global vision with robust down-home wit."
                - Gene H. Bell-Villada

WE SHOULD HAVE KILLED THE KING
by J.G. Eccarius $5.00
"A picaresque novel for the Baby Bust Generation. The book
opens in England in 1381 when Jack Straw and Watt Tyler were
hung for leading a rebellion of the serfs ... and casts forward a
bit into the future to describe what an anarchist society."
                - Flatland
"... anywayz, i really thought this was a kool book, i was freaked
out after I finished it. Be sure & read this!"
                - Iron Feather Journal

@ SAMPLES   edited by Bill Meyers $2.00
A collection of current day anarchist writings on the environment, literature, and community defense.

Send cash, check or money order to III Publishing, P.O. Box
170363, San Francisco, CA 94117-0363. Please include $1.00 for
shipping the first book, and $.50 for each additional book.
Foreign orders: include $2.00 shipping per book.